*It was his only chance to escape. . . .*
*A telephone . . .*

T.J. pressed the receiver to his ear. "Help!" he yelled into the telephone. There was no reply.

He poked 9-1-1 a second time. He heard nothing. No voice. No dial tone. T.J. jiggled the receiver holder and listened again. Nothing. The telephone was out of order.

A hand clamped down on T.J.'s shoulder.

## Books by Peg Kehret

Cages
Horror at the Haunted House
Night of Fear
Nightmare Mountain
Sisters, Long Ago
Terror at the Zoo
FRIGHTMARES™: Cat Burglar on the Prowl
FRIGHTMARES™: Bone Breath and the Vandals
FRIGHTMARES™: Don't Go Near Mrs. Tallie
FRIGHTMARES™: Desert Danger
FRIGHTMARES™: The Ghost Followed Us Home
FRIGHTMARES™: Race to Disaster
FRIGHTMARES™: Screaming Eagles
FRIGHTMARES™: Backstage Fright

Available from MINSTREL Books

# Peg Kehret

# Night of Fear

A MINSTREL® BOOK

Published by POCKET BOOKS
New York   London   Toronto   Sydney   Tokyo   Singapore

*Special thanks to Rosanne Lauer,*
*a thoughtful and perceptive editor,*
*whose skill always improves my work*

This book is a work of fiction. Names, characters, places and incidents are products of the author's imagination or are used fictitiously. Any resemblance to actual events or locales or persons, living or dead, is entirely coincidental.

 A Minstrel Book published by
POCKET BOOKS, a division of Simon & Schuster Inc.
1230 Avenue of the Americas, New York, NY 10020

Copyright © 1994 by Peg Kehret

Published by arrangement with Cobblehill Books

ISBN: 0-671-89217-7

First Minstrel Books printing October 1996

10  9  8  7  6  5  4  3  2  1

A MINSTREL BOOK and colophon are registered trademarks of
Simon & Schuster Inc.

Cover art by Mark Garro

Printed in the U.S.A.

*For my grandson,*
*Eric Carl Konen*

*April 18, 1992*

# Chapter One

*"Cluck, cluck, cluck!"*

T.J. Stenson glanced toward the source of the chicken imitation and quickly looked away. He wished the after-school activities bus would hurry. Why was it always late on the days when Craig Ackerley decided to hassle him?

"Here comes your pal, Ackerley," Dane whispered.

"Some pal," T.J. said.

*"CLUCK! Cluck, cluck, cluck. CLUCK!"* Craig tucked his hands into his armpits and flapped his elbows as he approached.

T.J. ignored him. So did Dane.

Craig quit clucking and flapping when he reached T.J. and Dane. "Hey, Stenson. I'm talking to you."

*I hear you, Craig,* T.J. thought. *I wish I didn't, but I hear you.*

"Why don't you grow up?" Dane said.

1

"What are you, his bodyguard?" Craig said. "Is Stenson such a baby that you have to protect him from big, bad Craig?"

"What do you want now?" T.J. asked.

"I see you got another *A* in English," Craig said. "Don't you know you're setting a bad example? How are the rest of us supposed to look good when you keep getting *A*'s all the time?"

"Sorry about that," T.J. said. "I tried to flunk, like you, but I just couldn't pull it off."

Dane snickered.

"Sorry about that," Craig mimicked. "Well, don't let it happen again. Hear?"

T.J. looked down the street again, relieved to see the yellow hulk of the school bus in the next block.

"I asked you a question, wimp." Craig put his face close to T.J.'s and glared at him. "Hear?"

"I hear. I hear."

"All right, then. It's a deal. No more *A*'s."

"There's just one problem," T.J. said.

"Yeah? What's that?"

"If I don't get *A*'s in English, I have to quit basketball."

"Huh?"

"No more *A*'s, no more basketball."

"Says who?"

"My parents. They mean it, too. If my grades drop, I'm off the team." *And if I'm off the team, turkey, you won't win half as many games.*

"Bye-bye, District Championship," said Dane.

Craig scowled. "In that case, you're excused this time. But the next time I talk to you, you jump." He punched T.J. on

2

the shoulder, just hard enough to sting. "Unless you want to fight," he said.

"He doesn't want to fight you," Dane said, as the bus sputtered to a halt. "He hates to see big boys cry."

Dane got on the bus and T.J. quickly followed. Craig did not ride the school bus home, thank goodness.

As the door creaked shut, Craig leered through the window at T.J. "I'll get you tomorrow," he yelled, "and I won't be the one who's crying." He began flapping his arms again.

The bus pulled away; T.J. blew his breath out.

"What's his problem?" Dane asked. "Why does he always try to start trouble with you?"

"Who knows? I avoid him if I can but he keeps showing up, trying to pick a fight."

"Maybe he's jealous because you're a better basketball player than he is."

"Maybe."

"Or maybe he just has a mean streak. I wonder what would happen if you punched him once. If you stand up to him and call his bluff, he might leave you alone."

"And he might beat me to a bloody pulp. He's two inches taller and outweighs me by thirty pounds."

"True. I'd be scared to fight him, too."

"Grandma Ruth used to tell me, 'Win with your wits, not with your fists.' So far, I've managed to outsmart Craig and avoid a fight."

"Is it true that your folks will make you quit basketball if your grades drop?"

"No. I just made that up to get Craig off my back about my grades."

Dane chuckled. "It worked."

"He'll find something else to complain about."

After Dane got off the bus, T.J. thought about what Dane had said about being scared to fight. Am I scared of Craig, as Dane thinks, or just being sensible? Or both? Sensible or not, he didn't like his buddy to think he was a coward.

When the bus stopped at T.J.'s corner, he hurried home, eager to get in some free-throw practice before dinner.

T.J.'s mother was in the kitchen. The house smelled like warm peanut butter cookies. This was the best part of having his mom quit work: she had plenty of time to bake cookies.

"I have a great idea," Mrs. Stenson said, as T.J. poured a glass of milk and helped himself to a handful of cookies. "Let's have a birthday party for you."

T.J. stopped chewing. This was the worst part of having his mom quit work: she had plenty of time to think about him.

"You could invite all the boys on your basketball team," she said.

"I don't think so."

"It would be a chance for your father and me to get to know them. I saw Mrs. Ackerley in the grocery store today and she said Craig is on the team and I thought, why, I haven't seen Craig Ackerley since you boys were in second grade."

An image of Craig, leering and yelling through the bus window, flashed across T.J.'s mind. He wished *he* had not seen Craig Ackerley since second grade, either. He wondered what Craig had in mind when he said, "I'll get you tomorrow."

"The Ackerleys bought one of those new houses on the other side of the swamp, in that Forest Ridge development. As the crow flies, we're practically neighbors."

4

"It's nice of you to offer, Mom, but I really don't want a birthday party this year."

"But . . ."

"The truth is, Craig and I don't have much in common anymore. His older brother hangs out with a group that's into drugs and alcohol, and Craig brags that he goes with them."

"Are you sure?" Mrs. Stenson looked shocked. "The Ackerleys seem like such nice people."

"Maybe they are, but Craig is a jerk." T.J. added what he knew would be the most convincing argument of all: "He has the worst foul mouth in the whole school."

"Oh." Mrs. Stenson was quiet for a moment as she digested that piece of news. "Well, of course, you could invite anyone you want. It wouldn't have to be the entire basketball team." She brightened. "Maybe you'd like a co-ed party. We could make it a barbecue."

T.J. examined his fingernails as his mother enthusiastically continued. "You can plan the menu; we'll have all your favorite foods. I could make that good baked bean dish that you like so much and maybe some potato salad, and cake, of course. A chocolate birthday cake, with fudge icing." She smiled at T.J. "And thirteen candles."

T.J. knew his mother was trying to please him but he wished she would quit trying. He said, "I don't want a birthday party. Thanks, anyway."

"Except for Dane, you never have your friends over anymore. It would be fun. And Dad and I would keep Grandma Ruth in her room. We'd see that she didn't embarrass you."

"It isn't because of Grandma Ruth," T.J. said, which wasn't true. He *would* be embarrassed if Grandma Ruth decided to count her play money or sing hymns in front of his friends, but he couldn't stand to shut her away in her room, either, as if he was ashamed of her. He wasn't ashamed but it was hard to make people understand that Grandma Ruth wasn't this way before she got sick. It seemed disloyal, somehow, to let other people watch her confusion if they could not remember how she used to be.

"Why don't you at least think about it before you decide?"

"All right. I'll think about it." But T.J. knew that he wouldn't change his mind. He remembered too clearly how Dane had reacted the first time he came over after Grandma Ruth moved in.

T.J. and Dane had been best friends since first grade so Dane had known Grandma Ruth when she was well and living in her small mobile home on the back of the Stensons' property. But he had not seen her during the two years she had lived with her other daughter, T.J.'s Aunt Marion.

Dane knew that Grandma Ruth had Alzheimer's disease; he knew it affected her brain. He even knew that Grandma Ruth's mobile home had been sold because she could not live by herself anymore, but he still could not conceal his shock the first time he saw her count her play money and heard her talk about long-ago people and events as if they were in the present.

Although Dane had not said anything, T.J. could almost hear him thinking, Man, she's really gone crazy, hasn't she?

Now, Dane was used to Grandma Ruth's odd behavior and he always said *hello* to her but T.J. was in no hurry to have other, more casual, friends over.

T.J. finished his cookies, got his basketball, and went outside to practice. He needed to keep up his free-throw skills. Even muscleman Craig backed off when T.J. threatened to quit the basketball team.

The Pine Ridge team's opening game against Lincoln was the next day. Their coach was confident that Pine Ridge had a chance to win the District Championship this year. The team had been good from the first day of practice and kept getting better. Two new boys, brothers, had just joined the team: Allen and Nicholas. They were tall and well coordinated and T.J. could tell they were going to be good team players. Not like Craig, who took too many shots himself instead of passing the ball to someone in a better position.

T.J. dribbled the basketball across the driveway and leaped in the air for a slam-dunk shot. Mentally, he heard the crowd cheer. As he went after the rebound, a horn honked directly behind him. Startled, T.J. missed the basketball and it bounced off the driveway into the bushes. While he retrieved it, his father opened the garage door and parked the car.

"There's been another fire," Mr. Stenson declared, waving the evening newspaper at T.J. "Just on the other side of Ridge Road. A tractor shed burned, with the tractor still in it."

"Arson again?" said T.J.

His father nodded. "The police say there's a pattern," he said. "They think the same person is responsible for more than a dozen fires."

T.J. carried the basketball to the free-throw line that was marked by two small stakes on either side of the driveway. He bounced the ball twice, aimed at the basket, and shot.

His father watched the ball swish through the hoop before he opened the door and called, "Amelia! There's been another fire."

T.J. shot one more basket and then went inside, too. His parents stood before the television set, their faces reflecting shock. Grandma Ruth sat near them, examining the play money in her purse.

T.J. asked, "What's happened?" but his father motioned for him to be quiet so they could hear the newscast.

T.J. looked at the screen and gasped, "That's *our* bank!"

His parents nodded silently.

"I'll buy flour today," Grandma Ruth said. "I need to bake bread."

T.J. stared as the newscaster gave details. *The man held a gun on the teller while she pushed cash across the counter to him. After grabbing the money, he pulled the trigger and then ran out of the bank.*

T.J.'s mother covered her mouth with her hand. The color drained out of her face.

*The teller was taken by ambulance to Cascade Hospital, where she was pronounced dead on arrival. Her name was not released, pending notification of her family.*

"Murder," said Mr. Stenson.

Mrs. Stenson nodded. She had tears in her eyes.

"Bank robbery and murder," Mr. Stenson said.

"Is it time for church?" Grandma Ruth asked.

"No, Mother," Mrs. Stenson said.

*Bank employees described the man as thirty to thirty-five years old, with dark hair, wearing jeans and a T-shirt. The man was last seen driving east on Ridge Road in a dark-colored truck.*

T.J. felt as if someone had just kicked him in the stomach. He had seen hundreds of news reports of robberies and murders, but it was different when the crime happened in a place he knew well. Just yesterday, he had gone with his mother to cash a check at the Pine Ridge Bank. He had stood in the lobby, in the very spot where a man had shot one of the clerks.

"I wonder which teller it was," Mrs. Stenson said.

In his mind, T.J. saw the smiling faces of the women who worked at the small branch bank. He didn't want it to be any of them.

"We can't be late for church," Grandma Ruth said.

"It isn't Sunday," Mrs. Stenson said. "We aren't going to church today."

"I'm going." Grandma Ruth stood and put on her hat, a broad-brimmed straw hat, with blue ribbons hanging down the back. Years ago, Grandma Ruth had pinned clusters of yellow artificial daisies all around the brim. The bright daisies always gave her a jaunty, youthful look, despite her gray hair and lined face.

Grandma Ruth began walking around the sofa. She moved in slow, deliberate circles, around and around the sofa.

T.J. wished she would stop it. It drove him crazy when she walked in circles like that.

Mr. Stenson, still watching the TV, shook his head in disbelief. "Murder!" he said. "Right here in Pine Ridge."

*One of the other tellers was also hospitalized, suffering from shock,* said the annoucer. *In other local news . . .*

9

T.J.'s father clicked off the television.

Grandma Ruth continued to shuffle around the sofa.

"I can hardly believe it," Mrs. Stenson said. "A murder, practically in our own backyard. I hope the police catch him quickly."

T.J. hoped so, too. It gave him a creepy feeling to think there was a murderer on the loose in his neighborhood.

# Chapter Two

"Why would he shoot her?" T.J. said. "If the bank teller gave him money, why wouldn't he take it and run?"

Mr. Stenson shrugged. "People who rob banks are not rational," he said. "He's probably on drugs."

Mrs. Stenson moved toward the kitchen. "Our dinner's ready," she said. "We'd better eat while it's still hot. We're having tacos."

Normally, tacos were T.J.'s favorite meal, but his appetite had disappeared.

"Come and sit down, Mother," Mrs. Stenson said. "It's time to eat your dinner."

"I don't want to be late for church," Grandma Ruth said.

Mr. Stenson patted her arm reassuringly and led her to her chair. "You won't be late. You have plenty of time."

Grandma Ruth smiled at him and sat. She said, "Thank you, David."

David was Grandma Ruth's brother, dead more than ten years. Mr. Stenson never corrected her when she called him David. He never corrected her when she called him Edward, either, apparently thinking he was her late husband. When that happened, Mr. Stenson only smiled sadly and patted her hand.

She occasionally thought T.J. was David, too. When she called him that, he either didn't answer or he told her his name. He refused to pretend he was David. He didn't even remember his Great Uncle David. Besides, he couldn't stand it when Grandma Ruth didn't know who he was.

He couldn't stand having Grandma Ruth talk about church all the time, either. Not that he had anything against going to church but it was out of character for Grandma Ruth. As a young woman, she left the church of her childhood and had never again attended any organized religious service.

When T.J. was old enough to be curious about her beliefs, she explained that, although she didn't follow a particular doctrine, she tried to lead a loving and moral life. "All the world is my church," she told him, "and my daily life is my religion."

In recent months, however, she frequently said she was going to church. She had taken to singing hymns, too, and T.J. was thoroughly tired of hearing them.

The Grandma Ruth that T.J. loved used to sing "You Are My Sunshine" and "How Much Is That Doggie in the Window?," complete with a realistic bark. Where did she go? T.J. wondered. What happened to the *real* Grandma Ruth? Who was this odd, befuddled stranger who clutched her purse and sang "Holy, Holy, Holy"?

T.J.'s mother said that Grandma Ruth sang hymns and talked about going to church because she sometimes slipped back in time to when she was a child. "Grandma Ruth grew up on a farm," Mrs. Stenson explained, "and the church provided her main social activities. She enjoyed church, especially the music."

"She isn't a little girl anymore."

"In her mind, sometimes she is. She goes back and forth, somehow, to different times in her life. Because she was poor as a young mother, she insists on always carrying a purse full of money now. And her childhood memories make her want to go to church."

It isn't fair, T.J. thought. She can remember something from sixty years ago but she can't remember what day it is now. And she can't remember my name.

When Grandma Ruth started singing hymns or counting her play money, T.J. usually left the room. His parents humored her, sometimes even pretending to be in church. They said if it made her happy, what was the harm?

A few months ago, they had taken her to a Sunday service but Grandma Ruth talked out loud during the sermon, called the minister David, and created such a disturbance that they had to leave. They had sat near the front, so Grandma Ruth could hear, and T.J. thought the walk back up the aisle, with the whole congregation watching, would never end. He had wanted to shout, "She wasn't always this way. She has a terrible brain disease." Instead, he stared at the floor, his cheeks burning.

T.J. wanted Grandma Ruth to be the way she used to be —vibrant and laughing, always interested in what T.J. did

13

and thought. When she used to call him on the telephone, she never asked the dumb questions that most adults ask kids, like, "What did you do in school today?" Grandma Ruth asked, "If you could have lunch with anyone in the world, who would it be?" or "Who do you think will win the World Series?" And she always listened to T.J.'s replies.

When T.J. was small, Grandma Ruth read books to him and played what they called hide-and-sneak. When he got older, she often invited him to spend Friday night at her house. They would play Monopoly and make milk shakes and eat pizza at midnight. In the morning, they read the sports page and then T.J. always made pancakes. Grandma Ruth had let him cook breakfast since he was seven years old and she didn't hover over him, watching every move, either. She just set the table and poured the orange juice and told him what a treat it was to have a man in the kitchen, for a change.

Back then, she never called him David. Back then, she knew exactly who he was. Back then, she didn't have Alzheimer's disease.

"I wish we didn't have to go to that school meeting tonight," Mrs. Stenson said, as she passed the plate of tacos.

T.J.'s attention returned to the conversation.

"I thought you liked Open House for the parents," Mr. Stenson said.

"I do. I just don't like leaving T.J. and Mother here alone."

"We'll be OK, Mom," T.J. said. "You leave us alone all the time."

"Not when there's been a murder in the neighborhood."

T.J. wished the Open House was a different night, too, but since it wasn't, he did want his parents to attend. His basketball coach planned to tell them about a basketball camp that was scheduled for next summer and T.J. thought he'd have a better chance of getting permission to go if his parents heard about the camp from his coach, rather than from him.

"That bank robber is probably in the next state by now," Mr. Stenson said. "We can't cancel the rest of our lives and cower in a corner."

"I suppose not," Mrs. Stenson said, though she still looked worried. "We won't be late," she told T.J., and then added, "Keep the doors locked."

"I will."

After his parents left, T.J. started his homework. He wanted to finish so he could watch *Top Gun* on TV. *Top Gun* was his favorite movie and, although he could practically recite the script by heart, he never missed a chance to see it again.

Grandma Ruth entertained herself by dusting the same table over and over. She hummed a hymn as she worked. After ten minutes or so, she began to sing the words. "Holy, holy, holy."

"Will you please sing something else?" T.J. said. He felt edgy tonight, and cross.

Grandma Ruth stopped singing and looked at him.

"Why don't you sing 'You Are My Sunshine' for a change?"

"I don't know that song."

"Sure you do." T.J. began to sing: "You are my sunshine, my only sunshine. You make me happy, when skies are gray."

Grandma Ruth looked blank. It was clear she did not remember the song she and T.J. had sung together hundreds of times when he was small.

She's the one who had taught the song to him. She always changed the lyrics and sang, "You'll never know, T.J., how much I love you." How could that be erased from her mind?

T.J. quit singing and returned to his homework. He had enough trouble with biology without trying to sing at the same time.

Almost immediately, Grandma Ruth began to sing again. "Holy, holy, holy. Lord God Almighty."

"Stop it!" T.J. said, his voice coming sharper than he had intended.

Grandma Ruth broke off in the middle of a note. "What's wrong, David?" she asked.

"I can't concentrate when you're singing," T.J. said. "I'm trying to do my homework. And *please* quit calling me David."

T.J. was perfectly capable of concentrating. He often did his homework with the TV on or with his stereo turned up to full volume, especially when his parents weren't home. It wasn't Grandma Ruth's singing that bothered him, it was the choice of songs. She sang the same few hymns over and over and over, and each time it reminded T.J. that Grandma Ruth was slowly losing her mind. I will never, he thought, for the rest of my life, be able to hear "Nearer, My God, To Thee" or "Holy, Holy, Holy" without wanting to cover my ears and run.

Grandma Ruth, looking hurt, sat down on the sofa and opened her purse.

"And don't count your money, either," T.J. said. "It's the same amount you had ten minutes ago. You counted it then."

"I need to be sure I have enough." Grandma Ruth removed the stack of bills and started putting them, one at a time, in a pile beside her. "We need eggs," she said, "and milk for the girls."

It was pink, green, and yellow money from T.J.'s old Monopoly game. Grandma Ruth counted carefully, making sure no bills stuck together.

T.J. sighed and returned to his homework. Sometimes he wished Grandma Ruth could leave this earth the way his other grandma had. One day Grandma Doris was the picture of health, planning a trip to the Grand Canyon, and the next day she was dead in her chair, from a heart attack, with the crossword puzzle beside her.

It had been a terrible shock but it was still better than this. At least Grandma Doris had been *herself* right up to the end. She had not left her body behind while her mind and personality went to some dark, unknown place where no one, not even her family, could follow.

"Good," Grandma Ruth said. She put the money back in her purse and snapped it shut.

When T.J. looked up, she smiled at him, a loving childlike smile, full of trust. Guilt settled like a cape on T.J.'s shoulders. How can I wish she would die? he thought. It isn't her fault she's like this. What's the matter with me?

"Is it time to go to church?" Grandma Ruth asked.

T.J. slammed his book shut and stood up.

The telephone rang.

"T.J., this is Edna Crowley. We've had car trouble and aren't home yet. Can you be our critter sitter one more time?"

The Crowleys were the Stensons' closest neighbors. Their house, an old barn, and a large pasture adjoined the Stensons' five acres on the west side, although it wasn't visible because of the thick stand of alder trees along the property line.

Since they both retired last year, Mr. and Mrs. Crowley took frequent short trips and they always hired T.J. to care for their dogs and cats. It was a good job. T.J. enjoyed playing with the animals and it didn't take long to walk across the back field, let the dogs out of their pen for a run in the pasture, and set out fresh water and food. He had gone twice a day all week but he had not gone that afternoon because the Crowleys were supposed to get home.

After assuring Mrs. Crowley that he would take care of the animals, T.J. got his sweatshirt and Grandma Ruth's coat. She would have to go with him; she couldn't be left alone, even for a short time. The last time Grandma Ruth was home alone, she turned all the stove burners to High and they were all glowing red when T.J.'s parents returned.

"It's a miracle she didn't burn herself," Mrs. Stenson had said.

"Or set the house on fire," Mr. Stenson added.

When questioned about it, Grandma Ruth said only, "It was time to cook Edward's dinner."

The phone rang again; this time it was Dane.

"Did you know *Top Gun* is on TV tonight?" Dane said.

"I'm planning to watch it but I have to go feed the Crowleys' animals first."

"Better hustle," Dane said, and hung up.

That's one thing T.J. liked about Dane. He never wasted time.

T.J. said, "Put your coat on, Grandma Ruth."

"Are we going to church?"

18

"We're going to see the baby kittens."

A stray cat had produced a litter of kittens in the Crowleys' old barn last month. T.J. had taken Grandma Ruth to see them once before and she had enjoyed the fuzzy babies.

Her crinkled face broke into a smile and she followed T.J. out the door.

It took him three times as long to cross the field when Grandma Ruth was with him as it did when he was alone. She stepped slowly through the long grass, carefully avoiding any stones. She kept pausing to look back, as if wondering where she was.

"Keep walking," T.J. said. "We have to hurry tonight."

"Where's David? Shouldn't we wait for David?"

"David isn't here," T.J. said crossly.

Grandma Ruth stopped. "Where is he?"

"Come on, Grandma Ruth," T.J. pleaded. "You're going to make me miss the opening of *Top Gun*."

Grandma Ruth headed back home. "I have to get David," she declared.

"Forget David," T.J. said. "David is dead."

Tears filled Grandma Ruth's eyes. "David died?" she said. "What happened? Oh, my. This is terrible news."

"It isn't exactly news," T.J. said. "It happened ten years ago."

But Grandma Ruth wasn't listening. She stood in the middle of the field with her arms folded, hugging herself. Grief was etched across her face.

When will I learn to keep my mouth shut? T.J. thought. He hadn't meant to make her unhappy, only to make her hurry. At least she wouldn't be sad for long. She'd soon forget what

19

he had said and ten minutes from now, she would be talking about David again, as if he were alive and walking beside her.

"Grandma Ruth," T.J. said. He touched her arm to get her attention and repeated her name. When she looked at him, he said, "We're on our way to feed the baby kittens. If we don't go, the kittens will be hungry." He held out his hand.

Grandma Ruth put her hand in his. It felt frail, like the body of a baby bird. She allowed him to lead her the rest of the way across the field and through the alders. When they reached the metal gate in the fence surrounding the Crowleys' pasture, T.J. grasped the handle with both hands and shoved. He kept forgetting to bring along a can of oil; it took all of his strength to slide the bar across so the gate would open.

The two dogs, Pepper and Salt, ran in joyful circles when they saw T.J. They were always more interested in getting petted than in being fed and T.J. scratched their heads and talked to them before he let them out to run in the pasture.

Grandma Ruth wandered over to the barn.

"Don't open the door until I get there," T.J. said. "We don't want the kittens to get loose."

Grandma Ruth sat on a big rock, opened her purse, and began to count the play money.

When the dogs were back in their pen, T.J. got dog food from the covered container that was next to the Crowleys' back door. He fed the dogs, filled their water bowl, and then joined Grandma Ruth.

When she saw him coming, she said, "Is that you, David?"

"No," T.J. said, trying not to sound annoyed. "I'm not David. I'm T.J."

Grandma Ruth walked with him to the barn door and waited

for him to open it. With one hand, she picked at the peeling paint that curled from the door frame. "This doesn't look like a church," she said. "Are you sure we're in the right place?"

"We're here to feed the kittens, Grandma Ruth."

He slid the wooden door open. The barn had not been used for horses since the Crowleys' daughter grew up and moved away, and the interior had a stale odor of mildew.

The inside of the barn was dark and T.J. fumbled along the edge of the door, feeling for the light switch. As he flicked it on, he turned toward the bales of hay where the kittens slept.

A man leaped to his feet, blinking in the sudden light. Bits of hay clung to his dark hair.

T.J. knew instantly who it was.

# Chapter Three

The description fit perfectly: jeans, dark hair. Under his open jacket, T.J. saw that he wore a T-shirt. He looked younger than thirty, but T.J. wasn't much of a judge of age.

T.J. grabbed Grandma Ruth's hand.

The man crouched. One hand groped on the floor behind the bales of hay.

"We didn't mean to wake you," T.J. said. "We were going to feed the kittens but we can come back later." He began backing toward the door, pulling Grandma Ruth with him.

"Are you the preacher?" Grandma Ruth said.

"We can't stay, Grandma Ruth," T.J. whispered. He took another step backward.

If he were alone, he would flick the lights off and run for it. He'd cut across the field and under the fence and get home and call the police. But he'd never make it with Grandma

Ruth. She was too slow. And he couldn't leave her here with a murderer.

The man found what he was feeling for. He jammed it in the pocket of his jacket. When he stood up, he kept his hand in the pocket. The pocket bulged and T.J. was sure the man's hand was closed around a gun, the same gun that had shot and killed the bank teller.

"Stay right there," the man said.

"He doesn't look like a preacher," Grandma Ruth said. "He isn't wearing a necktie."

"Hush, Grandma Ruth."

"What am I going to do with them?" the man said. "They'll have the cops on my tail before I get six blocks." He spoke as if there were someone else in the barn.

T.J. looked quickly around the barn but saw no one else.

"I don't know what you're talking about," T.J. lied. "Like I said, we just came to feed the kittens. If you needed a warm place to sleep for a few hours, I don't see anything wrong with using this barn. Why would we call the police?"

The man raised one eyebrow. "I can't let you stop me now," he said. "If you call the cops, I won't be able to finish." His hand moved inside his jacket pocket.

"My parents are waiting for us," T.J. said. "We live right next door. If we aren't back in a few minutes, they'll come looking for us."

The man frowned.

"We're going to church," Grandma Ruth said. "They didn't want to come."

"Then they won't be expecting you back in a few minutes. Nice try, kid."

"She's mixed up," T.J. said. He pointed to his jeans and sweatshirt. "Do I look like I'm going to church? We came to feed the kittens."

"I want my revenge," the man said, "and I won't let you stop me."

"Where's the organ?" Grandma Ruth said. "I want to sit near the organ."

"We won't stop you," T.J. said. "You can leave." He didn't even want to guess what sort of revenge the man meant.

A gray and white kitten darted out of a horse stall and ran to the bale of hay beside the man.

Grandma Ruth yanked her hand free from T.J.'s grasp and stepped toward the kitten. "Here, kitty, kitty," she said.

Instantly, the man moved closer to Grandma Ruth and put his hand on her shoulder. Ignoring him, she sat on the hay and tried to pick up the kitten.

T.J. thought fast. According to the newscast, the bank teller died en route to the hospital. The man wouldn't know that. He wouldn't know if he was wanted for murder or not. If he knew he was already wanted for murder, what difference would it make if he killed somebody else? But if he thought the teller had lived, he might think twice about pulling the trigger again.

"The bank teller lived," T.J. said. "She's doing great. The bullet just nicked her."

The man seemed not to hear. "I have to get out of here," he said, brushing the hay from his clothing.

"Look," T.J. said. "Why don't you just leave and I'll pretend you were never here in the first place. I don't have any reason to be mad at you and by the time we get home, Grandma Ruth will have forgotten all about you."

The man shook his head. "No," he said. "It's too risky. I can't take a chance on you running to the cops. You'll have to go with me."

Go where? For how long?

The kitten eluded Grandma Ruth's grasp and scampered away.

"This is an odd church," she said. "There aren't any pews." She spread her skirt neatly about her knees, folded her hands in her lap, and began to sing. "Holy, holy, holy."

"What's with her?" said the man.

"She has a brain disease. She gets confused and can't remember things. She thinks she's in church."

"Lord God Almighty," sang Grandma Ruth.

"My truck's just behind the barn. You and the nutty saint get in. You're coming with me."

"You can't take her! Half the time, she doesn't know where she is or even who I am. If you leave her here, she won't tell anyone about you. I swear it. She won't remember."

The man hesitated.

"If she's with us," T.J. said, "she'll attract attention."

"OK. OK, we'll leave her. Let's go."

"I have to lock up the dogs first." The lie rolled easily off his tongue. "Otherwise they'll follow us. They'll run after your truck."

"What dogs?"

"The dogs that guard this property. I let them out of their pen just before I came in the barn and I have to put them back in." If he could just get out the barn door, he could race home, call the police, and race back. Maybe then he could stall the man a little longer, and the police would find them while they were still here at the Crowleys. Even if he had to leave with the man in his truck, the police would know exactly what area to search. They would put up road blocks.

"There are guard dogs out there?"

"I have to lock them back in their pen."

"Well, make it fast. I'll stay with the saint while you do it."

One of the kittens batted at Grandma Ruth's shoelace. She laughed and wiggled her foot.

T.J. turned toward the barn door. How long would it take him to sprint home, call the police, and run back? Six minutes? Seven? Could he be gone that long without making the man suspicious? He would have to run faster than he ever had before. It was the only way to get help.

As if he could read T.J.'s mind, the man said, "Don't try anything funny. If you aren't back here in three minutes, this old saint's going to need last rites."

T.J. gulped. There was no way he could make it across the field to his own house and back in only three minutes. He didn't have a key to the Crowleys' house or he would call from there.

"Put those dogs in and come right back. Nothing else."

T.J. nodded. As he eased out the barn door, the man still stood directly behind Grandma Ruth. The hand in the jacket pocket was next to the gray curls that showed beneath her straw hat.

Grandma Ruth smiled as a kitten jumped into her lap.

T.J. closed the door behind him and bolted toward the dog

pen. Salt and Pepper met him at the gate, leaping and wagging. T.J. opened the pen and put them in the pasture. They galloped happily away.

If his parents saw the dogs there instead of in their pen, they would know something was wrong. They would come to investigate. So would the Crowleys, when they got home.

T.J. knelt in the dirt beside the doghouse. With his finger he scratched, HELP   BANK ROBBER   TRUCK.

He couldn't take time to do more. He had used at least two minutes already.

He wondered how long it would take his parents to look for him at the Crowleys' house. They still thought Mr. and Mrs. Crowley were coming home today. They had no reason to think that T.J. would come over to feed the animals.

If only he had left a note, telling his parents where he and Grandma Ruth were. He and his parents always left each other notes, if they went somewhere. But he had thought he would return long before his parents got home from Open House. There had been no reason to write a note.

T.J. ran back to the barn. Grandma Ruth waved when she saw him. "Hello, David," she said. "Did you come to see the kittens?"

"Let's go," said the man.

"Where's the preacher going?" asked Grandma Ruth. "Aren't we going to sing the hymns?"

"The preacher and I will be back soon," T.J. said. "Stay right where you are, Grandma Ruth. You're . . . you're in charge of the hymns today and I want you to stay right there and sing until we get back. Don't leave, no matter how long we're gone."

"Move it," said the man, as he shoved T.J. toward the door.

T.J. stumbled out the door. If Grandma Ruth stayed in the barn, she would be safe. Eventually, she would be found and taken home. If she wandered off, anything could happen to her. One of the remaining wooded areas in Pine Ridge County started on the other side of the Crowleys' driveway and Grandma Ruth could easily get lost in the woods. She could fall and break a bone and not be found for hours.

If she went the opposite direction, away from the woods, toward Ridge Road, there were other dangers. Cars drove too fast all over the Pine Ridge area and Grandma Ruth no longer remembered things like stopping to look before you cross a street.

His mind darted from one terrible possibility to another. Despite recent development, there were still coyotes in the region and as their feeding grounds shrank, they had begun attacking household pets. T.J. didn't think they ever attacked humans but he wasn't sure.

If the coyotes weren't a threat, the people were. Groups of rowdy teenagers used the privacy of the woods at night to drink and smoke pot. T.J. had seen news reports of elderly people in other cities who were robbed and beaten by drunken gangs who chose helpless victims. If it could happen elsewhere, it could happen here. There had already been a murder; any other horror seemed possible, too.

"You're in charge of the hymns!" he shouted. "Don't leave!" He shoved the barn door shut, wishing there was a latch or hook or some other way to lock Grandma Ruth inside.

He looked around the Crowleys' yard for a shovel or a piece

of lumber that he could use to brace the barn door so it wouldn't open. He saw nothing that would work.

"Come on. Quit stalling." The man grabbed T.J.'s arm and yanked him toward the back of the barn where a rusted blue pickup truck sat beside the bushes. A canvas tarp, fastened with a rope, covered something in the back of the truck. For one awful instant, T.J. wondered if it was the body of the bank clerk but then he remembered that she had died at the hospital.

As T.J. climbed in the truck, he heard Grandma Ruth's thin voice from inside the barn, singing, "Holy, holy, holy. Lord God Almighty."

The man put the key in the ignition. The starter ground briefly and quit. He tried again. T.J. crossed his fingers. Maybe the truck wouldn't start.

The engine caught, died, and caught again. That time, the man gave it more gas and they lurched forward toward the Crowleys' driveway.

"Put your head down," the man said.

T.J. leaned forward, his head on his knees. He felt the truck bounce along the Crowleys' private lane to the street and then turn left, toward Ridge Road.

# Chapter Four

After a few minutes, T.J. started to sit up.

"Keep your head down."

T.J. glanced at the man and then did as he was told. He wasn't sure if the man was afraid T.J. would signal for help or if he just didn't want T.J. to know which way they were going.

The truck seat bounced and jiggled. The man turned so many times that T.J. gave up trying to tell where they were.

Twice the truck stopped briefly, as if at a stoplight. T.J. wondered if other vehicles were stopped next to them. What would happen if he suddenly sat up and waved and yelled for help? T.J. lifted his head slightly.

"Stay down," the man growled.

"I'm getting stiff," T.J. said.

"You'll live."

The truck never went very fast and after several more turns, T.J. wondered if the man had a destination. He didn't drive like someone who needed to escape. Although he must know that every cop in the county was looking for him, he seemed to drive aimlessly, as if he had all the time in the world and was enjoying the scenery.

"Where are we going?" T.J. asked.

"None of your business."

"They'll be looking for me. My parents have called the cops by now."

"They won't know where to look."

"You can't keep me hostage forever. My folks will put my picture in all the papers and on the TV news. Somebody's sure to recognize me."

"Who said anything about holding you hostage?"

"What *are* you going to do with me?"

"I'll think of something."

T.J. glared at the man. "What's your name?"

"Brody."

"Is that your first name or your last name?"

"What is this, some sort of quiz? You want to call me by name, Brody is all you need to know."

"Have you ever been in jail?" T.J. asked.

"No! And I'm never going to jail, either. What do you think I am, some kind of criminal?"

"That's what most people would say."

"Well, most people are wrong. I never stole anything and I never hurt anybody in my life."

"You don't call it stealing to rob a bank?"

"Don't talk crazy."

"And the teller. I suppose you didn't hurt that bank teller."

"I don't know what you're talking about."

"Yes, you do. I saw the TV news. It showed the bank and the ambulance and one of the nurses at the hospital."

"You're crazy, boy. You're talking out of your head."

"Me? *I'm* crazy?"

"That's what I said. I don't know about any bank robbery so don't go getting it into your mind that I do."

"Denying the truth won't make it go away."

Grandma Ruth had told him that, when he was five years old and accidentally broke his mother's favorite flower vase. Grandma Ruth found him burying the pieces in his sandbox.

"Denying the truth won't make it go away," she said.

T.J. shoveled more sand on the pieces of vase.

"Go tell your mother what happened," she advised him.

"She'll spank me."

"No, she won't. Not if you say it was an accident and tell her you're sorry."

He took her advice and was astonished when his mother hugged him and praised him for being honest. After that, he tried never to deny the truth.

*Keep singing, Grandma Ruth. They'll find you soon.*

"I'm not denying the truth," Brody said. "I'm opening some eyes so the truth is known." He spoke with pride, as if he had been chosen by the President for an important assignment.

"When I'm done, the whole world will know the truth of what it was like for me."

T.J. squinted in the darkness, trying to read the man's face. "What exactly do you mean?" he asked.

"Where were the cops when I needed them? Looking the other way, that's where. Well, they won't keep looking the other way when I'm finished."

The man's voice rose as he talked, taking on the desperate quality that politicians got when they tried to convince people that they were the only ones who could save the country from disaster.

Finished with what? T.J. wondered. The more Brody talked, the more unbalanced he seemed. T.J. remembered his dad saying the bank robber was probably on drugs. Maybe he was still high on something. He certainly sounded like a cokehead. Or maybe he was nuts. Or both.

Great, T.J. thought. I'm riding around, going who knows where, with a lunatic on drugs behind the wheel.

T.J. listened for traffic noise but heard nothing except the rattling of the truck itself.

"I'm getting a kink in my neck," T.J. said.

Brody glanced out the windows in all directions. "All right. You can sit up."

As he did, the truck stopped at a red light. T.J. looked out the window at an abandoned grocery store, the sort of small Mom-and-Pop kind of store that used to be on Ridge Road, before the supermarket came. The store's windows were boarded over and NO TRESPASSING was scrawled in large black letters on a crude wooden sign.

He had no idea where they were. The only other building he saw was an old house with a faded sign out front: AN-TIQUES. Diagonally across the sign was another sign that said, CLOSED.

Next to the house was an empty lot with a chain-link fence around it. Whatever had stood on the lot was now demolished and T.J. suspected the antique shop and the grocery store were next in line for the wrecking ball. Dead leaves and crumpled papers clung to the bottom foot of the fence as if trying to climb over and escape.

"Come on, come on," Brody said to the red light. He looked in the rearview mirror and drummed his fingers on the steering wheel.

On the far corner of the old grocery store, blending in with the dirty exterior of the building, T.J. saw a phone booth. Without stopping to think, he flung open the door of the truck, leaped out, and sprinted toward the phone booth.

Behind him, Brody yelled, "Hey!"

In his haste, T.J. tripped on the curb and nearly fell. He stumbled, slowed, and managed to get his balance. Without looking back, he ran across what used to be the grocery store's parking lot.

He zigzagged as he ran, in case Brody took a shot at him. He hadn't thought about the gun when he jumped out of the truck, which, he realized, was a stupid mistake. Still, it was dark now and T.J. was fast, and a moving target was hard to hit.

He reached the phone booth and pulled on the door handle. Nothing happened. T.J. yanked harder; the door was stuck shut.

T.J. put his shoulder against the rusted hinge in the center of the door and shoved. The door gave slightly. He stepped back, lifted his foot and kicked at the hinge, hoping he wouldn't shatter the glass and cut his ankle to shreds. His heel hit right on the hinge, so hard that it sent ribbons of pain up T.J.'s leg, but the hinge gave way, and the door opened.

He stepped inside the phone booth, grabbed the receiver with one hand and punched 9-1-1 with the other. It was a good thing the emergency number was always a free call, because T.J. had no money with him.

Even with the door open, the phone booth smelled like moldy earth and dried urine. T.J. tried not to breathe the stale air.

As he put the receiver to his ear, he looked to his right, through the dirty window of the phone booth, trying to see a street sign or something else that would indicate where he was so he could tell the emergency operator where to send help. He saw only the abandoned buildings.

He looked to his left. Across the empty parking lot, he saw the blue pickup, sitting in the street with both doors wide open. A car, driving in the opposite direction, slowed while the driver looked at the truck. Then the car picked up speed and continued.

T.J. pressed the receiver to his ear. "Help!" he yelled into the telephone.

There was no reply.

He poked 9-1-1 a second time.

He heard nothing. No voice. No dial tone.

T.J. jiggled the receiver holder and listened again.

Nothing. The telephone was out of order.

A hand clamped down on T.J.'s shoulder.

It came to Dane in a flash: the perfect way to get Craig Ackerley to quit bothering T.J. He would videotape Craig being obnoxious and then show the tape in Communications class.

As one of the school's roving reporters, Dane was supposed to film ordinary scenes at random, edit them, and present a fifteen-minute video each Friday afternoon. The class loved seeing themselves and their friends; they called Dane's presentations "The Pine Ridge Candid Camera."

Until now, Dane had shown only clips that made people look good. His aim had been to catch people unaware as they picked up litter, or told a funny story, or held a door for someone whose arms were full of books. But now he intended to be ready and the next time Craig started in on T.J., Dane would start the video camera.

Dane knew what would happen if the whole Communications class saw Craig's disgusting behavior. They would jeer and boo and give Craig a bad time about it. Craig would be so embarrassed that he would quit bothering T.J.

Dane waited until *Top Gun* stopped for a commercial and then dialed T.J.'s number, eager to share his idea. He planned to assume a false voice when T.J. answered and say, "This is Mr. Fogbrain, head of the English department at Pine Ridge School. It has come to my attention that your grades have slipped and therefore you are suspended from the basketball team."

But Dane never got to say his little joke because no one answered the phone at the Stensons' house.

That's odd, Dane thought. He knew T.J. would watch his favorite movie. Well, maybe T.J. was in the bathroom or outside, calling his cat, Fluffy, home. He would try again later.

T.J.'s arm shook as he hung up the pay phone.

He turned to face Brody

"I called 9-1-1," he said. "I told them where we are. The police will be here any minute."

A flicker of fear shone for an instant in Brody's eyes. He reached past T.J. and grabbed the telephone. "I'll cancel the call," he said. "I'll tell them it was a practical joke."

He stretched the metal telephone cord taut across T.J.'s shoulder and leaned forward to put his ear to the receiver.

For the first time, T.J. noticed that Brody wore a small gold earring in one ear. T.J. didn't remember the television newsman mentioning an earring when he broadcast a description of the killer; the bank employees must not have seen it.

Brody reached past T.J. to flick the receiver holder up and down. A slow smile formed. "You didn't call anybody," he said. "Not on this phone."

He dropped the receiver. It clanked twice against the back of the phone booth and then dangled helplessly.

Brody yanked T.J. out of the phone booth and shoved him toward the street where the truck sat.

T.J. looked in all directions, hoping another car would come along. The street was deserted.

T.J. got in the truck. Brody closed the door and climbed in the other side.

"That was a stupid thing to do," Brody said. "You might have got hurt, jumping out like that. You don't want to get hurt, do you?"

"No."

"All right, then. You do as I say from now on."

T.J. nodded.

Brody started the truck. "Down," he said.

"I won't jump out again."

"Down!"

T.J. bent forward and put his head on his knees. Next time, he would think it through before he made a move. He shouldn't have tried it when there were no other people around. He should have waited until there was another car nearby, or people who would hear his shouts and rescue him.

The truck hit a chuckhole in the street. T.J. bounced, hitting his head on the dashboard.

He wondered what time it was. There was a clock on the dashboard of the truck but it didn't work. Open House at school didn't last long so his parents should be getting home soon. Any minute now, they would discover that he and Grandma Ruth were missing. Maybe they already had. Maybe the Open House got over early. His parents might already be looking for him.

He hoped they would call the neighbors first. They might think he had gone over to the Crowleys' house to collect his pay and stayed to visit awhile, to hear about their trip. Maybe, when nobody answered at the Crowleys', his parents would go over there. They would see Salt and Pepper out in the pasture and know something was wrong.

Maybe by now his parents had found the message in the dirt. Even if they didn't find the message, they might look in the barn, because the kittens were part of T.J.'s job. Or they might hear Grandma Ruth singing.

As soon as his parents opened the barn door and saw Grandma Ruth, they would know T.J. was in trouble. They knew that T.J. would never leave Grandma Ruth there by herself. If his parents found Grandma Ruth in the barn, they would call the police immediately. The cops were probably hunting for him already.

The parents at the Open House talked more about the robbery and murder than they did about their childrens' progress in school. Everyone was horrified that such a violent crime had happened in their neighborhood.

"We need to organize a Crime Watch program," someone said. "If we don't, this kind of thing is going to occur more and more often."

Several people decided to meet at Denny's after the Open House, to discuss ways to keep the neighborhood safe. The Stensons were invited to attend.

"We told T.J. we'd be home right after the Open House," Mrs. Stenson said.

"I'll call him," Mr. Stenson said, "and let him know we'll be late."

Mr. Stenson went to the pay phone in the hallway near the school office. There was no answer.

"Maybe we should go straight home," Mrs. Stenson said, "just to be sure everything is all right."

"T.J. probably has the volume on his stereo turned up again and can't hear the telephone," Mr. Stenson said. "I don't know how he can stand to have it so loud. I've told him he'll ruin his hearing."

"Sounds like my son," said one of the other parents.

"He only does it when we're gone," Mrs. Stenson said, "and Mother doesn't mind. She doesn't seem to notice that it's full volume. Her hearing isn't as sharp as it used to be."

Mr. and Mrs. Ackerley, Craig's parents, came by on their way to their car. "Are you folks coming to the meeting at Denny's?" Mr. Ackerley asked.

"I'm a bit nervous about T.J. and his grandmother," Mrs. Stenson said.

"I know what you mean. We left our two boys by themselves tonight, too, but that's all the more reason to help start a Crime Watch program. With a good neighborhood plan in effect, there would be less cause for nervousness."

"You're absolutely right," Mr. Stenson said. "Come on, Amelia."

When the Stensons arrived at the restaurant, the other parents were speculating about where the bank robber might have gone. Mrs. Stenson went to the phone at the front of the restaurant and dialed home again. She let it ring ten times before she hung up.

When she joined her husband and the others, Mr. Stenson gave her a questioning look.

"Still no answer," she said.

"Remember the day we tried to call him from the airport,

when the plane we were meeting was so late?" Mr. Stenson said. "We called and called and there was never any answer and we were sure something was wrong. When we finally got home, he was right there in the den, listening to his music. He didn't hear the phone. He didn't hear us come in the door."

Mrs. Stenson nodded. She had been so certain that other time that T.J. was sick or injured, and so relieved when he was perfectly all right. No doubt it would be the same tonight; T.J. had his stereo volume cranked up to High and would be surprised to learn that they had tried to call him.

"That pecan pie sounds too good to resist," Mr. Stenson told the waitress. "I'll have it warm, with ice cream."

"I'll have the same," Mrs. Stenson said.

# Chapter Five

One hundred miles east of Pine Ridge, in a service station near the freeway, Mr. and Mrs. Crowley, T.J.'s neighbors, listened while a mechanic explained what was wrong with their car.

"How long will it take you to fix it?" Mr. Crowley asked.

"Not long. An hour or two."

"Good. We'll go get a bite to eat and come back."

"Better not come until after breakfast tomorrow," the mechanic said. "It won't take me long to fix it, but I can't get the part I need until morning."

Mr. Crowley looked at his wife and sighed. "We'd better find a motel," he said.

"I'll have to call T.J. again," Mrs. Crowley said. "He'll need to feed the animals tomorrow morning, too." She put the call on her credit card and let it ring a long time before she hung up.

"We can try again after we eat," Mr. Crowley said.

T.J. rode in silence, hoping to hear sirens at any moment. By now, he thought, Mom and Dad are home. Maybe the Crowleys are home, too. They've found Grandma Ruth and called the police and every cop in the state is searching for me.

Soon a squad car will pull us over. Soon Brody will see blue lights flashing in his rearview mirror and hear the shrill scream of the highway patrol car's siren. Soon this nightmarish ride will end.

He listened and listened but he heard only the rattling of the old blue truck.

Grandma Ruth sang "Holy, Holy, Holy" three times. She sang "The Old Rugged Cross" twice. She sang "Nearer My God To Thee."

She was going to sing "Holy, Holy, Holy" again but her throat was getting scratchy. She needed a cup of tea or a drink of water.

She looked around the empty barn. She wondered why David didn't come. Or had he been here and left? Was he waiting for her at home? She couldn't remember.

Putting her hat on the floor, she lay down on the hay to rest. Before long, she shivered. It was cold in this church and she couldn't think why she was here. The preacher had left long ago. She decided to go home and fix herself a bowl of nice, hot vegetable soup. That would take the chill from her bones.

Grandma Ruth stood, stretched, and walked to the door of the barn. She had to use both hands and push with all her strength to make the door slide open. She stepped outside, surprised to see that it was dark out. She had better hurry. Edward would be home from work and wondering why there was no dinner on the table. Her husband was a patient man, but he did like his meals served on time. She closed the door carefully behind her and set off down the road.

Pound, pound, pound.

T.J. heard a dull, steady noise.

The truck was idling again. Another red light, no doubt. T.J. moved his neck from side to side, trying to work the kinks out.

Pound, pound, pound. He strained his ears, trying to figure out what the throbbing sound was. Pound, pound.

A stereo! The pounding noise was the bass notes of a stereo. Every nerve in T.J.'s body was instantly alert, as if he had just been plugged into an energy socket. If there was music nearby, there had to be people. Kids, probably, walking along with a boom box. Or another car, with the radio volume turned up so high that the bass notes carried right through the closed windows of the truck.

The noise seemed to come from his left. T.J. sat up, looking quickly in that direction. Through the window on the driver's side, he saw the source of the music. A minivan was stopped beside the truck, waiting to make a left turn. The driver of the

44

minivan nodded his head and snapped his fingers in time to the music. He didn't look toward T.J. and the truck.

"Get back down," Brody said.

T.J. ducked down again. His mind sped faster than a downhill skier in the Olympic Games. He could jump out. He could hitchhike to a telephone and call the police.

But what if Brody whipped the gun out of his pocket the second T.J. opened the door? What if he fired one, fatal shot before T.J. ever had a chance to ask the minivan driver for help?

I'll have to move fast, T.J. decided. He inched his head up just far enough to see the traffic light turn yellow.

He jumped out of the truck, slammed the door behind him, and, crouching low, ran around the back of the truck. As he went past the back of the minivan, he banged on the rear window.

The music was louder now, a heavy rock beat that swirled in the air around T.J.'s head. The minivan driver swayed in time to the beat.

T.J., still crouching so he was out of Brody's sight, reached up and thumped on the driver's window.

The light turned green.

T.J. stood up. "Help!" he cried. "Let me in." He tried to open the door but it was locked.

The blue pickup drove away.

The startled minivan driver peered through his window at T.J.

T.J. banged again.

"Hey, man!" the driver said. "Knock it off."

"Help!" T.J. said. "I need help."

The driver reached toward the dash and turned a knob. The music stopped. He rolled his window down an inch.

"Give me a ride," T.J. pleaded. "I need to get to a phone, to call the cops."

"Where'd you come from, kid? What you doin' out here all alone at night?"

"Can't I tell you after you let me in? I can talk while you drive."

"I'm not lettin' some stranger in my car without a good reason. What do you think I am, crazy?"

"You saw that blue pickup that was next to you?"

The driver nodded.

"That guy robbed a bank today and killed the teller. He was hiding in my neighbor's barn and I found him and he made me go with him. I jumped out just now, while he was stopped at the red light. He'll probably be back for me any minute. Please! Let me come with you."

The driver stared at T.J. for a moment. His eyes were narrow, as if he were thinking about what T.J. had said.

"What bank?" he asked.

"Pine Ridge Bank. He still has the gun in his pocket."

The man shook his head. "You're pretty young to be involved in some kind of scam," he said.

"This *isn't* a scam. I need help!"

"Sorry, kid," the driver said. "I just listened to the news and you weren't kidnapped by any bank robber."

"It wouldn't be on the radio yet about me being kidnapped," T.J. said. "It just happened a little while ago."

The man pointed a finger at T.J. "I don't know what you're tryin' to pull, kid, but you aren't pullin' it on me."

He cranked the window back up. He reached for the radio knob and the rock music came back, full volume. The minivan took off. It turned left, accelerating quickly.

"Wait!" T.J. shouted. He ran after the van, into the middle of the intersection, but it was clear that the driver wasn't going to stop.

Why didn't the man believe him?

He couldn't stand there and wonder why. He had to get away, in case Brody came back, looking for him.

T.J. ran to his right and started down the sidewalk. At least, he thought, I got away from the murderer in the pickup. I may not know where I am but wherever it is, it's better than being in that truck. Another car is certain to come along soon. They don't have traffic lights in areas where there isn't any traffic. Or I'll come to another phone booth, one that works.

He jogged along, past a used bookstore, a yarn shop, and a child-care center, all of which were closed. He'd gone less than a block when he heard a vehicle approaching from behind him. He looked over his shoulder as he ran but he was looking directly into the headlights and couldn't tell what kind of vehicle it was.

Should he dart alongside one of the buildings and hide, in case it was Brody? Or should he take a chance that it was someone else, someone who could help him?

Maybe the minivan driver had thought it over and had a change of heart. Maybe he realized that T.J. didn't look like the sort of person who would be involved in a scam so he went around the block and came back. Maybe it was a different car altogether, with a driver who would help him.

There was a big chestnut tree on the boulevard just ahead. T.J. ducked behind it. If the headlights belonged to the old blue truck, he was hidden. If it was some other vehicle, he could jump out and yell for help as it went past.

When the headlights were almost even with the tree, T.J. peeked around the front of the tree and prepared to leap out. As the lights passed, T.J. saw that they belonged to a white sedan. He jumped from behind the tree, waving his arms and shouting.

"Stop!" T.J. yelled. "I need help!"

The car never even slowed down. He could tell there were three passengers, in addition to the driver, but not a single one of them turned to look back at him. They didn't see him running along the sidewalk after them. They were so busy talking to each other that they didn't hear him yelling.

He couldn't possibly run fast enough to catch the car. Panting, he slowed to a walk.

Minutes later, he saw headlights approaching again. This time, he decided not to wait until the vehicle was past before he yelled for help.

When the headlights were half a block away, T.J. ran to the curb and tried to get the driver's attention. The headlights came faster.

T.J. stepped off the curb, waving his arms over his head like signal flags. "Stop!" he yelled. "Stop!"

The old blue pickup stopped.

Brody got out.

T.J. turned and ran.

"Hold it right there." Brody's voice was steady. Menacing.

T.J. stopped. No matter how much he wanted to escape, he couldn't risk his life. There was no truck and no minivan to hide behind now. Earlier, when he ran to the phone booth, Brody didn't shoot but that time, he was caught off guard. That time, T.J. had been zigzagging across the dark parking lot before Brody could get out of the truck and aim the gun.

This time, Brody was only a few feet away, just as the bank clerk was only a few feet away when she was killed. If Brody shot the bank clerk for no reason except that she could identify him, he might do the same with T.J.

"Get back in the truck."

T.J. still didn't see the gun but Brody had his right hand in his pocket again. T.J. wondered if the bank clerk saw the gun before it went off. He tried to remember exactly what the TV newsman had said. Did the witnesses describe a weapon or only the sequence of events? He couldn't remember and right then, it really didn't matter. T.J. did as he was told.

"Head down."

T.J. put his forehead on his knees but he kept his head turned so he could watch Brody.

Brody didn't drive off right away. He sat there and looked at T.J., as if wondering what to do with him. Finally, he spoke. "What did the guy in the van say?"

"He didn't believe me when I said I needed help. He thought it was some kind of scam."

Brody nodded his head. "It figures."

"Why did you drive off?"

"I couldn't be sure what that driver would do. I left, in case he helped you, and I came back, in case he didn't."

"Well, he didn't."

"Nobody ever helps."

"I want to go home. My parents will be worried about me."

"You can't go home. If you went home, you would tell them about me."

"No, I wouldn't. I swear I wouldn't! I wouldn't say anything about you. I'd say I was at my friend Dane's house and didn't realize how late it was. They would believe me."

Brody shook his head. "You would tell," he said sadly, as if T.J. had already betrayed him. "You would tell all about me and then they'd know who to look for and I would never finish my revenge."

"But I have to go home eventually. If I don't, the police will be looking for me. You'll get caught sooner because I'm with you than you would on your own."

Brody nodded. "We'll hurry," he said. "I'll do as many as I can tonight." He started the truck.

As many as he can? Brody talked as if he planned to break into more banks tonight.

"You'd move faster if you didn't have to keep chasing after me," T.J. said.

"I'm not going to chase you anymore."

What does that mean? T.J. wondered. The next time I run, you'll let me go? Or the next time I run will be the last time my legs carry me anywhere?

"If you leave again, I'll go back to the barn and get the nutty saint. She won't run from me."

# Chapter Six

When Grandma Ruth reached the junction where the Crowleys' private dirt road joined the street, she stopped. This wasn't the way she had come. She and David never walked on paved streets. They always followed the deer trails through the woods or they cut through Papa's cornfields, with the high stalks brushing their shoulders. The only time they saw paved streets was when Papa and Mama took them into town.

A car whizzed toward her. The driver, glimpsing Grandma Ruth on the side of the road, honked the horn. Grandma Ruth stepped away from the sudden noise and shut her eyes to close out the bright lights.

When the car passed, she turned and went back toward the barn.

Before she got there, she saw a metal gate shining in the moonlight. It looked familiar. Had David brought her through that gate? No, that wasn't David; that was T.J.

She stopped walking. T.J. Her only grandchild. She had not thought it was possible for her ever again to love anyone as much as she loved Edward, her late husband, or her daughters, Amelia and Marion. But, oh, she did love T.J. She hadn't seen him for a long time; she wondered where he was. Was he still a small boy or had he grown up when she wasn't looking and become a man? Children had a way of doing that. One day her Amelia was sitting on her lap, listening to stories, and the next day, or so it seemed, Amelia had a baby of her own.

Grandma Ruth walked until she reached the gate. Two large dogs saw her coming and jumped against the fence as she approached. They acted friendly and she thought she recognized them. Were they T.J.'s dogs? She seemed to remember T.J. feeding them. When she reached the gate, she stopped and looked across it at the empty field.

The field. Of course. She remembered now. Her house was on the other side of that field. Papa and Mama and David were all there, waiting for her to get home so they could eat dinner.

Grandma Ruth reached for the metal bar and tried to slide it, to open the gate, but it didn't move. She pushed and pushed, until the metal made a deep red mark in the palms of her hands but she couldn't budge it. She could not get into the field that she needed to cross to get home.

She would have to walk around, through the woods. Maybe she would find David there. Maybe he was waiting for her, with his berry-picking bucket. Or was it T.J. who used to pick those sweet little blackberries with her and then help her make jam?

She wondered why the preacher didn't come.

She put one hand on her head. Where was her hat? Had she left her hat at home, or forgotten it in the church? Nervously, she opened her purse and felt inside, to be sure she still had her money.

She walked away from the gate, passed the barn, and left the Crowleys' property. She crossed the lane and started into the woods. Surely she would find David soon. He was probably waiting for her just ahead, with his berry bucket.

As she walked, she hummed softly, "Nearer, my God, to thee. Nearer to thee."

The old blue truck picked up speed; T.J. could tell by the way the engine whined and the tires hummed.

T.J.'s nerves jangled. He wondered if his parents had found Grandma Ruth yet. He hoped so. She might get scared if she waited in the barn very long and nobody came.

Too bad Grandma Ruth wasn't the way she used to be. Five years ago, she would have been out of that barn and across the field to call the cops before T.J. and Brody had gone three blocks. Even three years ago, when she was first diagnosed but before she went to live with Aunt Marion, she would at least have been able to find her way home, and could have told his parents what had happened.

Not now. Now, Grandma Ruth lived in a world all her own. Once in awhile, the fog in her brain seemed to lift and she acted as if she understood but most of the time she didn't seem to know or care what went on around her.

As he had hundreds of times before, T.J. thought Alzheimer's disease was the most terrible disease there was. It would be better, he thought, to lose your sight or the use of your legs than to lose your mind. At least if Grandma Ruth was blind or paralyzed, she would still know who he was. She would still be able to carry on an intelligent conversation.

As he rode along, memories of Grandma Ruth as she used to be swept through his mind. Grandma Ruth taught him to ride his bicycle by running along, holding onto the seat and yelling, "Keep pedaling!" Grandma Ruth cheered at his grade school basketball games. Grandma Ruth helped him make gifts for his parents for Mother's Day and Father's Day: macaroni necklaces and wooden picture frames and herb gardens.

He remembered when she let him stay up past midnight to finish a good book, admitting that she sometimes did the same thing herself. He saw her shaking her fist at the politicians on TV, declaring she could do a better job of running the country than any of them did.

She used to make sandwiches and invite T.J. to have lunch in what she called "The World's Greatest Outdoor Restaurant." It was their own special hiding place on the back side of the woods, reached by walking on logs from fallen trees which were laid end to end to form a path across a broad swampy area. The swamp was L-shaped and when they were almost to the far side, the log path turned sharply, revealing a huge weeping willow tree on the other side of the swamp. Its long branches bent downward until the tips touched the ground.

Grandma Ruth and T.J. would part the branches with their hands, as if they were pushing aside strands of hanging beads, and enter The World's Greatest Outdoor Restaurant.

They always sat on the ground, with their backs against the

54

tree trunk, completely encircled by the hanging willow branches. Sunlight filtered through the leaves as they feasted on peanut butter sandwiches and oranges.

Grandma Ruth told him, "Restaurants try to create atmosphere by hanging a lot of plastic plants from the ceiling. If they really want atmosphere, they should plant a weeping willow tree in the middle of the dining area."

T.J. used to giggle as he imagined a huge tree growing in the middle of Burger King, taking up all the table space.

He had loved going to The World's Greatest Outdoor Restaurant and he knew Grandma Ruth had loved it, too. She didn't go because it was a way to entertain a small boy. She enjoyed it as much as he did.

That was one of the best things about Grandma Ruth—she could always create fun out of nothing.

Where had that bright, inventive mind gone? How could she be content to do nothing but count faded Monopoly money and sing a few old hymns, over and over and over?

One day shortly after Grandma Ruth moved in with the Stensons, T.J. had erupted in rage. "I don't want her to be this way," he shouted. "I want the real Grandma Ruth to come back."

"So do I," Mrs. Stenson replied, her eyes filling with tears.

"It isn't fair!" T.J. cried. "She's too smart to act so stupid."

"Smart people get sick, too," his mother said. "It's a tragedy for Grandma Ruth to be this way but we can't do anything about it. There is no cure for her, and no treatment. And it doesn't help her or anyone else for you to scream about it."

Later, T.J. felt ashamed of his outburst but the shame didn't change his angry feelings. All his life, T.J. had been proud of

55

Grandma Ruth. Maybe that's why it hurt so much to see her now. The contrast between what she used to be and what she had become made the loss unbearably painful.

"You can sit up now," Brody said.

T.J. straightened and looked out the window. He saw a freeway sign, "Echo Glen. Next Right." They were on Interstate 90, heading east. Brody kept the truck in the right-hand lane and when T.J. glanced at the speedometer, he saw that they were going exactly fifty-five miles per hour. Probably Brody didn't want to take a chance on getting stopped by the Highway Patrol for speeding.

*I wish the police would hurry and find me,* T.J. thought. The moment he had the thought, he heard, in his mind, Grandma Ruth's strong, youthful voice. "Wishing won't help. You must take action, T.J."

Her words had been spoken during one of T.J.'s Saturday visits, when he was nine. He had confided to Grandma Ruth that he wished he was a better basketball player.

"Wishing won't help," Grandma Ruth replied. "You must take action, T.J. Don't wait for good things to happen. Take action and *make* them happen."

"What kind of action?" T.J. asked.

"Think hard," Grandma Ruth replied. "What one thing could you do right now that would help you be a better basketball player?"

"I could grow six inches."

Grandma Ruth laughed. "That's beyond your control," she said. "What action can you take, today, this minute, that will help?"

"I could practice my free throws."

56

Grandma Ruth grabbed his hand and shook it. She patted him on the back as if he had just made a brilliant speech. "That's right!" she cried. "Practice your free throws today, and tomorrow, and every day after that, and I guarantee you'll become a better basketball player."

That same day, T.J. started spending an hour every afternoon, practicing free throws. Within a few months, he could sink them almost every time. His confidence grew and he decided to practice dribbling the ball, too, until he could dribble with either hand and switch the ball from front to back while he was running.

*Make it happen. Take action.*

What action could he take in this situation? Escaping from a crazy man with a gun was not the same as learning to play better basketball. Still, it didn't help to sit there like a blob of Play-Doh as he rode farther and farther from home.

I'll try to get him to stop, T.J. decided. I'll see if I can make him pull off the freeway, where there's more of a chance that someone will see us. If we stop near other people, I can signal for help.

"I have to go to the bathroom," T.J. said.

"You'll have to wait."

"I have to go bad. Can't we stop at a rest stop? Or a gas station?"

Brody didn't answer but at the next freeway exit, he turned off and drove to a gas station. There were no other cars in the station. A large sign said NO CHECKS ACCEPTED. An attendant sat inside, behind a window, and customers slipped the money for their gas through an opening beneath the window. T.J. reached for the handle of the truck door.

"Wait for me," Brody said. "I'm going with you."

They both got out of the truck.

"Don't say anything," Brody said. "Don't talk to anybody."

The door to the men's room was around the corner of the building. As T.J. walked toward it, with Brody behind him, he stared through the window at the attendant, hoping to catch the woman's eye, but the attendant just sat there, looking bored, staring at a small television set.

T.J. waited until Brody unzipped his pants. Then he bolted out of the men's room, tore around the corner of the gas station, and yanked open the door to the room where the attendant sat.

"Call the police," he said. "The guy I'm with is a murderer; he robbed a bank this afternoon and killed the teller and . . ."

The attendant leaped out of her chair and backed away from T.J., her eyes round.

"Where's the phone?" T.J. asked. He looked frantically around the small room. "We have to call for help. Quick!"

Brody raced around the corner of the building, dashed into the room and grabbed T.J. by the shoulder.

"I told you to stay with me," he said. "What are you doing, scaring this nice lady like that?" He looked at the station attendant. "It's hard to raise kids these days," he said. "Ran away from home just because his mother and I wouldn't let him buy a motorbike. She's worried sick about him." He dragged T.J. toward the door. "Come on, Billy. I'm taking you home whether you like it or not."

"He's lying!" T.J. cried. "Does he look like my father? He's no relation to me at all. He's a murderer!"

The attendant seemed terrified. She looked from T.J. to Brody and back again, as if wondering whom to believe.

Brody pushed the door open with his shoulder.

"Call the cops," T.J. pleaded. "Let them decide who's lying and who's telling the truth."

The woman reached under the counter and lifted out a telephone. As she did, another car pulled into the station. A tall man with gray hair, wearing a suit and tie, got out of his car.

"Help!" T.J. shouted through the open door.

The gray-haired man hurried over. "What's going on here?"

"My son ran away from home," Brody said. "I'm taking him back where he belongs before he gets himself in big trouble."

"He's the bank robber," T.J. said. "He's the one who killed the teller this afternoon at the Pine Ridge Bank. He isn't my father and I didn't run away. I found him hiding in my neighbor's barn and he made me go with him or else he was going to shoot my grandmother, the way he shot the woman in the bank."

As T.J. talked, Brody rolled his eyes, as if he had never heard such a wild story in his life. "Not true," he muttered. "Not true."

The gray-haired man patted T.J. on the shoulder. "Now, now, son," he said. "Calm down. Kids your age always think their parents don't know anything but you'll come to realize that they are only trying to do what's best for you. I remember when my boys were your age, they thought they knew everything, too. One even tried to run away once, but he came home soon enough."

Frustration bubbled and rose in T. J. like boiling spaghetti overflowing its pot. "What's the matter with you?" he said. "This guy robbed a bank and killed the teller and then he made me go with him and now he's making me go with him again. Why won't you believe me?" He clenched his fists, feeling as if the whole world were against him.

The man smiled. "Well, for one thing," he said, "I heard on my car radio that the police captured that bank robber a couple of hours ago. By now, he's locked behind bars."

T.J. stopped struggling with Brody and gaped at the man. "But they didn't catch him," he said.

"Oh, yes, they did," said the attendant. "I heard it on TV."

"You go on home with your dad now," the man continued, "and things will look better in the morning." He handed the woman a ten dollar bill. "I'm on pump number three," he said.

The station attendant took the money, slid the telephone back underneath her counter, and sat down. "You should be ashamed, Billy," she said, "telling lies about your father that way."

"My name isn't Billy; it's T.J.—and he isn't my father. There's been a mistake; the cops arrested the wrong man."

"Let's go, Billy," Brody said, as he shoved T.J. out the door.

T.J. stumbled toward the blue truck. Looking back, he saw the attendant and the gray-haired man nodding their heads and talking, as if agreeing that kids today can't be trusted to tell the truth about anything. T.J. opened the door, climbed in, and slumped against the seat.

If the police had arrested someone for the Pine Ridge Bank robbery and killing, then they would no longer be looking for a suspect with dark hair, wearing jeans and a T-shirt.

Brody climbed into the driver's seat. He reached across T.J. and locked the door on the passenger's side.

"That was a stupid trick," he said. "I told you not to talk to them."

Not that it did me any good anyhow, T.J. thought. How could this guy sound so unbalanced when he was raving on about getting his revenge and then be sharp enough to convince two strangers that he was T.J.'s father, trying to discipline an unruly son? He recalled the story of Dr. Jekyll and Mr. Hyde that he had read in English class last year. Maybe Brody had some sort of split personality.

"And what was all that about me robbing a bank and shooting some woman? I told you before I don't know anything about any bank robbery."

Maybe he's telling the truth, T.J. thought. Maybe the cops really do have the killer in custody. If so, who was this?

"What were you doing in the Crowleys' barn?" T.J. asked.

"Who?"

"Mr. and Mrs. Crowley, my neighbors. You were in their barn when I went in to feed the kittens."

"Oh, you mean when you found me. I was just taking a nap. Getting some sleep and waiting for it to get dark enough."

"Dark enough for what?"

"You'll see."

T.J. felt like slamming his fist into the dashboard.

61

Brody turned up the freeway on-ramp. T.J. looked over at him in surprise. Did Brody realize he was headed west, going back the way they had come?

"That name is a new one. T.J. I never heard that before."

"It stands for Ted, Junior. I'm named after my father."

My father.

T.J. leaned his head against the cool window and wondered what his father was doing at that very moment. Driving around the neighborhood, looking for T.J.? Sitting in the police station, filing a Missing Person report? Riding in one of the cop cars, searching around T.J.'s school? One thing for sure. Whether the killer was in custody or not, Dad was looking for T.J. by now. And Dad would do everything humanly possible to find him.

Back at Denny's, Mr. Stenson was glad he had gone to the meeting. This group of parents had a lot on the ball. Their ideas for keeping the area safe flowed freely and, even though a few of the suggestions were rather farfetched, plenty seemed workable. He noticed that his wife was taking notes.

When someone passed around a yellow tablet and asked everyone to write their name and phone number so they could be contacted for future meetings, Mr. Stenson was happy to sign up.

"More coffee?" the waitress asked.

"Just a half," Mr. Stenson said.

"Did you hear they caught the bank robber?" the waitress said. "It was on the radio a few minutes ago."

Sighs of relief were heard from around the table.

"I hope T.J. knows that," Mrs. Stenson said. "He seemed a little nervous when we left."

"He's probably watching his movie and hasn't heard a news report," Mr. Stenson said.

"If he's watching TV, he might hear the phone," Mrs. Stenson said. "I'm going to call him again."

One hundred miles away, in a room at the Pony Soldier Motel, Mrs. Crowley said almost the same words to her husband: "I'm going to call T.J. again." She sat on the edge of the bed and listened while the Stensons' telephone rang and rang and rang.

Mrs. Stenson went to the phone near the Denny's entrance, dropped her coins in the slot, and dialed. The line was busy. T.J. must be talking to Dane, probably discussing tomorrow's big game against Lincoln.

I shouldn't worry so much about T.J., she thought. He's almost thirteen years old and very responsible. Smiling, Mrs. Stenson hung up.

Mrs. Crowley hung up, too. "I'm going to bed," she said. "Those dogs won't starve if they don't get breakfast tomorrow."

Mr. Crowley agreed.

# Chapter Seven

T.J. looked at the gas gauge. The needle was between Empty and one-quarter full. All right, T.J. thought. We can't drive around much longer, without stopping for gas. If I can be patient, I'll have another chance to get help.

The truck slowed. Brody drove off the freeway and onto a service road. At the first corner, he turned left and followed a narrow, winding road up a steep hill. Buildings were infrequent and there were no streetlights.

The truck lurched to a stop. Brody rolled down his window and stared out. T.J. looked, too, trying to figure out what Brody was looking at. The moon was almost full, shedding a thin white light across the fields. T.J. could see rows of plants but he couldn't tell what the crop was. Some sort of winter vegetable. Cabbages maybe, or brussels sprouts.

On the far side of the field, T.J. saw a two-story farmhouse and, in the other direction, some outbuildings. T.J. breathed faster. Maybe he could get away and run to the farmhouse for help. This time, he wouldn't say anything about the bank robbery or the murder. He would just say he had been kidnapped. This time, maybe someone would believe him.

Brody shut off the truck's lights but not the engine. He sat for a few moments with the engine idling and then he turned onto the road that led toward the house. It wound through the fields, past a rusting old hayrake, and then branched into a *Y*, with the left side going toward the house and the right side going toward the outbuildings.

Brody turned right. The truck crept past a building that might have been for equipment storage and then past a barn. It stopped in front of a small shed. Moonlight glinted off the shed's corrugated-tin roof. The shed was painted white with bright blue trim. Pink poppies blossomed along the front.

Brody got out of the truck but left the engine running.

Too bad the truck doesn't have an automatic transmission, T.J. thought. Even though he had never driven, he could probably manage if he didn't have to shift.

Still, this was a chance to escape. T.J. slid slowly across the seat until he was behind the wheel. He looked over his shoulder; Brody was walking beside the shed, looking at the ground.

T.J. released the emergency brake, pushed in the clutch with his left foot, and tried to shift into Drive. The truck made a screeching sound, like fingernails being scraped across a blackboard, and promptly quit running. T.J. turned the key; the truck screeched again.

This isn't going to work, T.J. realized. Even if I can get it started, it's too dangerous to drive when I haven't a clue what

I'm doing. He quickly slid back to the passenger's side, surprised that Brody had not come out when the truck screeched.

Inside the shed, an animal whinnied. T.J. got out, opened the door of the shed, and looked inside.

Except for the patch of moonlight that shone through the open door onto the hay-covered dirt floor, it was dark in the shed. It took a moment for T.J.'s eyes to get used to the dark. He heard a movement to his right and saw a small pony, tethered in a stall. The pony's ears stuck straight up and his tail swished nervously. He looked at T.J., opened his mouth and whinnied again, showing his teeth.

"Hello to you, too," T.J. said.

A piece of the shed's tin roof flapped once in the wind and then lay still.

The inside of the shed was painted white, and a saddle, reins, and horse blanket hung in a tidy row on one wall. Inside the stall, T.J. saw that the pony had a clean bed of hay and a feeding trough that said FRISKIE in blue letters. A small table held brushes. Probably some kid's pet, he thought, as he closed the door.

Brody was walking next to the equipment shed. "Revenge," he said.

T.J. waited.

"Get in the truck."

They both climbed back in the truck. Brody made a *U*-turn. T.J. could hear Brody's breath coming quickly, as if he had been running. Neither of them spoke.

Brody drove back past the barn and the equipment shed and then stopped again. That time, he turned off the engine and pocketed the keys.

"Put your head down," Brody said. T.J. obeyed. "Don't make a sound. If you stop me, you'll regret it."

He got out.

T.J. heard noise at the back of the truck. It sounded as if Brody was untying the tarp. He waited a minute and then looked.

Brody was hurrying back the way he had just come, carrying what looked like a pail in his right hand. The moonlight reflecting off the tin roof of the shed acted as a beacon. T.J. saw Brody disappear inside the shed.

T.J. squinted at the door of the shed; Brody stayed inside. T.J. opened the truck door as quietly as he could, glad that the overhead light did not work. He listened. The loose piece of tin flapped twice on the roof. The pony neighed.

T.J. swung his legs to the side and slid off the seat. His feet touched the ground. His ears strained to hear if Brody was coming but he heard only the neighing of the pony, louder now. The animal clearly did not like Brody disturbing him.

At that moment, it occurred to T.J. that Brody might have left the gun in the truck. Was it still tucked into his jacket pocket, or was it lying in the truck where T.J. could get it? T.J. leaned back in, feeling quickly across the seat. When the gun wasn't there, he stuck his hand underneath the driver's seat, moving it back and forth, with his fingers outstretched. He found only a half-empty pack of cigarettes.

He straightened and looked into the bed of the truck. The tarp was pulled back, revealing a row of four red and yellow five-gallon gasoline cans, the kind the Stensons used to fill their power lawn mower. If they were full, Brody could drive a long time without needing to stop at a service station. T.J.

lifted one of the cans, intending to pour the gasoline out. It was empty.

Quickly, he lifted the other cans. They were empty, too.

T.J. walked away from the truck, toward the farmhouse. He wanted to run but he was afraid of making noise. He wanted a good head start before Brody discovered that he wasn't in the truck. He picked each foot up carefully and set it down gingerly, nervous that he would cause a twig to snap or a pebble to roll. Slowly, quietly, he walked farther from the shed, away from the truck. The pony neighed again, sounding frantic now. What was Brody doing back there?

With the pony making so much noise, T.J. dared to walk faster. When he judged that he was more than halfway to the house, he broke into a run, his arms pumping at his sides. Brody couldn't catch him now. He would easily make it to the house and get help. Even if Brody was already on his way back to the truck and discovered that T.J. didn't wait there, he couldn't catch up to T.J. now, not before T.J. got to the house.

Exultation made T.J. run even faster. Glancing back over his shoulder, he saw an eerie glow. It took a second for him to realize what it was.

The shed was on fire. Bright yellow fingers of flame reached out the open door, grasping at the edges of the tin roof.

The pony's terrified voice sliced through the night; the creature's fear sent a thrill of horror down T.J.'s arms. He remembered the dry hay on the ground, the wooden stall where the pony was tethered.

The pony neighed again. It was a higher pitch than before,

almost a scream. T.J. turned around and ran back toward the shed.

Back at the restaurant, Mrs. Stenson looked at her watch. "Goodness," she said. "It's nearly ten o'clock. We'd better be on our way."

Other parents murmured surprise that so much time had passed.

Mr. Stenson agreed that they should leave. But even after everyone gathered their coats and left a tip and paid the bill, the parents clustered in the parking lot, still talking about how they could keep their children safe.

When the Stensons finally reached their own driveway, the house was dark.

"It looks as if T.J. already got Mother to bed," Mrs. Stenson said. "I hope she didn't give him any trouble."

"You worry too much," Mrs. Stenson said. "T.J. is quite capable, when he has to be."

"I'm surprised he went to bed already, too. He was going to watch a movie on TV."

"Maybe he's in training for tomorrow's basketball game. Which reminds me: his coach told me tonight about a basketball camp that he'd like T.J. to attend. He feels T.J. is an extraordinary player, for his age."

"Oh?" Mrs. Stenson turned on a light in the living room and sat down. "Tell me about it."

T.J.'s feet pounded down the dirt lane, his breath coming in gasps now. He coughed, choking as he inhaled smoke.

Ahead of him, he saw flames darting through the open door of the shed.

As he approached the burning shed, he saw Brody standing off to one side, watching the fire. A gasoline can, like the ones in the back of the truck, sat on the ground beside him. Brody smiled, looking like the groom at a wedding or an athlete who had just broken a world's record. How could he stand there, looking so happy, when a helpless animal was about to be cremated alive less than twenty feet away? Did he plan to set the other buildings on fire, too?

T.J. didn't stop to ask questions. He drew in his breath, held it, and ran through the open door of the pony's shed. On his left, the flames were shoulder high. T.J. feared the wall on that side would collapse any second. To his right, the frantic pony pawed and kicked at his stall. The whites of the animal's eyes were enormous with fear. His lip curled up and he neighed over and over, with no pause in between.

The slight covering of hay on the dirt floor had burned itself out. The ground still smoldered but at least T.J. did not have to run through flames.

He looked over the top of the gate on the pony's stall and saw a metal latch that would allow the gate to swing open. He reached for the latch and then jerked away; the metal was so hot it burned his fingers. Instinctively, he stuck his singed fingers in his mouth and licked them.

He pulled the sleeve of his sweatshirt down over his hand and tried again. With the sweatshirt acting as a pot holder, he got the latch open.

Sweat ran down the back of his neck. He had to let his

breath out and inhale again. He held his arm up, trying to filter the smoky air through the sleeve of his shirt.

He kicked the gate open and saw that the pony was tied to the far side of the stall. T.J. stepped into the stall and fumbled with the pony's tether. The animal seemed to sense that T.J. was trying to help him. He quit jerking his head and stopped kicking at the stall. His eyes seemed to plead with T.J. to hurry.

The tether was knotted around one side of the stall. T.J. pulled frantically at the leather strap, trying to untie the knot. He was choking now and his eyes smarted and watered so much that he had to blink constantly in order to see what he was doing.

The tin roof crackled from the heat. Beside him, the wooden walls sizzled and spit like a steak on the broiler. The flames danced around the perimeter of the shed.

At last, the knot gave way. Grasping the tether in both hands, T.J. tugged, leading the pony out of the stall. When the frightened animal saw that T.J. was pulling him toward the burning wall on the other side of the doorway, he braced his legs and held back. Clearly, the pony did not want to go closer to the flames.

T.J. pulled. "Come on, Friskie. This is your only chance. There is no other way out."

The pony whinnied in terror and began to buck.

There was only one door. If they didn't get through it soon, it would be too late. The entire left wall of the shed was now on fire; soon there would be nothing left to hold up that portion of the roof.

Sparks exploded like a string of firecrackers across the interior of the shed. Dry hay in the pony's stall ignited.

The pony looked over his shoulder and saw the fire burning in the stall. T.J. tugged on the tether. The pony put his ears back, stopped bucking, and followed.

Just as T.J. pulled the pony through the door of the shed, the left half of the structure collapsed. With one side of the shed gone, the fire spread quickly through the rest. The dry wood of the door frame splintered and began to burn. Within seconds, the open door was a solid sheet of flame.

One minute later, T.J. thought, and the pony and I would both have been trapped inside.

The rest of the shed buckled inward and fell to the ground.

Ashes, smoke, and tiny bits of wood billowed toward the moon like an erupting volcano. The tin roof bounced slightly as it clanged to the ground.

The noise made the frightened pony bolt and the tether jerked out of T.J.'s hands. The pony galloped toward the farmhouse.

T.J. stood as if he were hypnotized, watching the fire.

Within seconds, the shed was gone. Only the blackened roof remained on the ground, with smoke pouring out from under it on all sides.

A bright flicker on the far side of the shed caught T.J.'s attention. Hot ash or a piece of burning wood must have dropped into dry grass.

He circled the smoking remnants of the shed. When he got to the far side, a small grass fire was spreading away from the pony shed, toward the barn. T.J. stamped on the flames, trying to get them out with his feet. Just as he got one spot out, the flames cropped up again a few feet away.

A grass fire, he knew, could be even more dangerous than the shed fire was. A grass fire, once it got out of control, could sweep quickly across many acres, laying waste not only the crops but everything else that stood in its way: equipment, vehicles, and even the farmhouse.

Three small fires erupted at the same time, a few feet apart. Sparks were obviously smoldering in the dry grass.

T.J. took off his sweatshirt and, holding tightly to the sleeves, beat at the flames.

Whack! Whack! The sweatshirt slapped the ground, smothering the fire beneath it. He could cover more ground at one time with the sweatshirt than he could with his feet. Smoke rose from under the sweatshirt and T.J. feared the material would catch fire, too, but it didn't.

Whack! Whack! T.J. flung the shirt again and again, until he thought his arms would fall off.

It worked. The burning grass smoldered and smoked but the flames died out, leaving only a charred black area on the ground.

T.J. stood still, his breath coming fast. His nostrils and throat felt raw from the smoke he'd breathed and he had a taste of smoke in his mouth, as if he had swallowed great gulps of it. He wiped his face with the sleeve of his sweatshirt, wishing he had a drink of cold water. He waited and watched, to be sure the fire didn't start up again.

Smoke hung thick and heavy in the air, making the night seem darker than before. The remains of the shed hissed and snapped as they settled to their final resting place.

73

When he was certain the grass fires were out, T.J. looked around for Brody. He was gone.

T.J.'s weariness lifted. Maybe I can still get away, he thought. With a fresh burst of energy, he ran the same way the pony had run: toward the house. Toward help.

As he approached the spot where the lane branched, he saw that the truck was still parked there. There wasn't any way to reach the house without passing the truck. T.J. narrowed his eyes, trying to see if Brody was behind the wheel. The truck appeared empty.

T.J. drew closer. When he was nearly to the spot where the road branched, Brody stood up. He had been sitting on the ground with his back against the truck's rear tire.

Brody stretched and took a step toward T.J. "Wasn't that something?" he said. He sounded awed, as if he'd just witnessed a glorious sunset or seen a bald eagle in flight. "My old man would be proud of that one."

T.J. slowed to a walk but kept moving. He passed the front of the truck. He turned, walking backward, so he could keep an eye on Brody.

"Get in," Brody said. "It's time to go."

"I'm not going with you anymore."

"I said, get in." The voice was harsh now.

"No!" T.J. backed away from Brody's outstretched hand. "You can go on by yourself. I'm staying here."

"Get in the truck!" The tone of Brody's voice was ominous.

T.J. hesitated. There had been no gun in the truck. Was there one in Brody's pocket? Maybe Brody didn't even have a gun. Maybe he had shoved something else in his pocket, back there in the Crowleys' barn.

Maybe, T.J. thought, I should run.

The pony whinnied again, this time from the direction of the house.

"Get in," Brody hissed. "Now." He grabbed for T.J.'s shoulder.

T.J. ducked, whirled around, and ran.

Brody instantly dove forward and his outstretched hands caught T.J.'s ankles, tackling him from behind.

Brody's fingers dug into T.J.'s ankles as T.J. landed face down in the dirt.

"You are asking for real trouble, boy," Brody said. He kept one hand on T.J. as they both stood up.

Whether he has a gun or not, T.J. thought, he's stronger than I am. He can force me to go with him and I'll just make it worse for myself if I run again.

Wearily, he returned to the truck and got in.

Grandma Ruth stumbled on a protruding tree root. She grabbed at a bush to steady herself and then quit walking. She looked in all directions but, no matter which way she turned, it seemed the same.

The woods had always been a joyful place, full of adventure and discovery. Now, for the first time in her life, she was unhappy here. She was tired, too tired to go another step. She decided to do as the animals do and make herself a nest in the dry leaves. She would curl up on the forest floor, like a fox or a fawn, and fall asleep.

Tomorrow, after she was rested, she would go home. Surely by morning, Edward would find her. He would hug her and take her home and tease her about her foolishness.

"How could you get lost in our own woods, Ruthie?" he would say. "You know every stone and leaf better than the squirrels who live here."

And she would laugh and tell him, "I wasn't lost. I just decided to spend the night with the deer."

Smiling, Grandma Ruth eased her weary body to the ground and closed her eyes. She heard only the slight rustling of the leaves as an occasional breeze brushed her face. It seemed as if she were the only person in the universe.

Then, not far away, she heard the yipping of a coyote and she felt less alone.

# Chapter Eight

Brody drove slowly away, with no lights.

Am I a coward? T.J. wondered. Did I give in too easily? I could have yelled, and struggled with him; someone might have heard us. If I had kicked him and bit him, I might have been able to get away and outrun him. Maybe Craig Ackerley is right. Maybe I am scared to fight. Maybe I am a wimp.

On the other hand, what if the police made a mistake and had the wrong man in custody? What if Brody did have a gun?

*Win with your wits, not with your fists.* I'm trying, T.J. thought. I'm trying, Grandma Ruth.

As the truck sneaked down the lane past the vegetable fields, T.J. looked back at the house. Light now glowed in an upstairs window. What were the people doing? Maybe they heard our voices or heard the pony, when it got near the house. Had they seen the fire? Had they called for help?

T.J. thrust his hand toward the steering wheel and pushed on the horn. It responded, barely, with a weak *beep* before Brody shoved T.J's hand away.

A yard light went on, flooding the front of the house with brightness. T.J. saw a man step outside and look in all directions before he ran down the porch steps and crossed the yard. A small child ran after him. At the far side of the yard, the pony waited quietly, the tether hanging from its neck. The man moved toward him. The pony stood still while the man and the child approached.

Despite his weariness and anger, T.J. smiled. The pony was safe. That was something. T.J. was riding around with a lunatic who burned down other people's property, but at least, because of him, the pony was alive.

Brody didn't turn the headlights on until he reached the main road.

T.J. watched for a police car or fire engine but none appeared. Surely the fire had been discovered by now. The man would try to put the pony back in the shed and would find the smoldering ruins. But there was no reason to call the fire department; the fire was already out.

Would the farmer call the police? Maybe not. He might think the fire started spontaneously. Or maybe he was glad to be rid of the little building. Maybe he could hardly wait to collect his insurance money so he could build himself a new, bigger shed.

Brody said, "I bet that one will be a shocker. Way out here, with their pretty garden and their open space, they won't be expecting it."

Something in T.J. snapped. "What's the matter with you?"

78

he said. "How could you stand there and let that poor pony burn to death? All you had to do was untie him. You could have turned him loose before you lit the fire."

Brody looked startled. "What pony?" he said.

"*What* pony? The pony I rescued. The pony that was screaming because it was tied in its stall while you set fire to the place."

"I didn't see any pony."

"You must have heard it."

Brody shook his head.

"Then you must be blind and deaf," T.J. said, "because there was a pony right inside the door, plain as day, and it was yelling its head off the whole time."

"When I'm getting revenge, the rest of the world fades away. Everything else disappears."

"And your revenge is to burn down other people's property?"

"My revenge is to make the rich people of the world pay attention, so they'll know what it's like for the rest of us."

"I doubt if those farmers are very rich." T.J. leaned his head against the seat.

"Their shed is gone now."

"It's gone," T.J. agreed, "and the people who owned it will get stuck cleaning up the mess and building a new shed." He looked at Brody. "I could have been killed, you know. It wasn't easy, getting that pony out before the shed collapsed."

"You went in the shed? You went in while it was burning?"

"There wasn't any other way to get the pony out." He glared at Brody. "And if I had been trapped inside, it would have been all your fault."

"Only a fool would run into a burning building. If you don't have sense enough to stay out of a fire, it isn't my fault."

"It's your fault that there was a fire to begin with. It's your fault that the pony was left in there." Memories of the thick smoke and the leaping flames made T.J.'s hands sweat. He had nearly lost his life and he would not soon forget the smell of that smoke or the terrified cries of the pony.

"I didn't push you in that door."

"What would you have done, if I had been trapped inside?"

"Nothing."

"Thanks a lot."

"I didn't even know you were in there. I told you, when I'm thinking about my revenge, everything else fades away." Brody glanced over at T.J. "Even if I had seen you, I wouldn't have done anything different. I'm not fool enough to go into a fire. Not me."

T.J. pictured himself trapped in the burning shed while Brody strolled happily back to his truck.

"Why did you go in?" Brody asked.

"I just told you. To rescue the pony."

"It wasn't your pony."

"What does that have to do with anything? No matter who it belongs to, I couldn't let it burn to death when all I had to do was untie it."

"Why not?"

"Because . . ." T.J. tried to think what to say that Brody would comprehend. He remembered when he was about three years old and Grandma Ruth caught him smashing ants with a rock. "You must be kind to all creatures, T.J. Each one is important; each has a special place on Earth."

"Ants don't."

"Oh, but they do." She explained that ants have lived on Earth for more than 100 million years. "They live in colonies," she said, "and each colony has a queen." She told him how hard the ants work and showed him an anthill, with the ants climbing in and out.

T.J. had been fascinated by the anthill and had spent several hours looking for the queen ant, expecting it to be wearing a tiny golden crown. After that day, he never again killed an ant intentionally.

T.J. looked at Brody. "All creatures are important," he said.

"Huh?"

"The pony deserved to live."

"It wasn't any use to you. You couldn't take it with us."

"That doesn't mean his life had no value."

"You're nuts. You know that? 'All creatures are important.' What kind of crazy talk is that? You're just as nutty as the saint back there, singing in the barn."

Sure I am, T.J. thought, and you are Citizen of the Year.

The more he thought about the pony, the angrier he got. Where he had initially felt only fear when he looked at Brody, now he felt rage. As the fury built in him, it pushed his fear of Brody away.

"Exactly what are you getting revenge for?" T.J. asked.

"The fire."

"What fire?"

"They burned my store."

"Who did?"

"All of them! I don't know who. They burned my store and

everything in it. People went crazy, running in the streets, smashing cars and setting fires. They burned my store."

T.J. had seen clips on the news of riots in different cities, with people looting and burning. Whole neighborhoods sometimes went up in flames. "Where were you, when it happened?" he asked.

"I was on my way home from a delivery when the trouble broke out," Brody said. "A gang surrounded my truck and wouldn't let me through. I finally abandoned the truck and walked home. Mobs of people were shouting and throwing rocks through windows and overturning cars. I couldn't believe it! The closer I got to home, the worse it was. They ran from one store to the next, smashing windows, helping themselves to the merchandise, and setting fires. All of the businesses in my block were owned by local people, like me. My old man opened that furniture store with money he earned as a janitor. Why would our own customers want to burn it down? Why would they destroy everything my old man had worked for?"

"It must have been terrible," T.J. said.

"I called for help," Brody said, "but nobody came."

"None of that is the fault of people around here. What good does it do to burn down this farmer's shed? He didn't do anything to you."

"I want everyone to know what it's like to have their property destroyed."

"Two wrongs don't make a right. Starting other fires won't get your store back."

"It will get me some attention. Maybe you people will notice what's going on in the world, for a change. You sit here in

82

your fancy houses, with your green lawns and your fresh air and you don't care what happens to the rest of us."

"That isn't true! People do care; we care a lot."

"Oh? Where was all that caring when my store burned down? I was left without any income—no money for food and no place to live. Did you care about that? No. Nobody cared except me."

"People try to help," T.J. said. "After the last earthquake in California, my school collected money and sent it to buy new books for a library that was wrecked. I worked at a car wash one Saturday and so did my friend, Dane, and we sent all of our profits to the library fund. And my parents sent money to help people in Florida after they had a hurricane."

"Well, nobody sent money to me."

"How could they? How could we have known that you needed it? You can't expect ordinary people to know who needs help. That's what agencies like the Red Cross and the Salvation Army are for. If you needed food, why didn't you contact them?"

"It's always been this way. Some people have more than they need and some never have enough and those who have the most won't share." Brody's voice had a fanatical sound, as if he were giving a well-rehearsed speech to a roomful of people.

"Do you think I'm rich?" T.J. said. "Is that why you're making me go with you? Because if you do, you are dead wrong. Since my mom quit work, my family barely has enough to pay our bills."

"You have a house, don't you? And food on the table?"

"Yes, but . . ."

"Then you're rich enough."

"Other people have had trouble, too. Practically every time I watch the news, there's a flood or a riot or a hurricane somewhere. You aren't the only one with problems. Somebody always needs help, somewhere."

"All the more reason to get revenge."

"Look," T.J. said, "I'm really sorry that your store burned down but why don't you rebuild it? You could get a loan, and start over. It would be a lot better than running around setting fires and ending up in jail." He glanced at Brody. "You *will* end up in jail, you know. Sooner or later, you'll get caught."

Brody's response was to drive faster.

The anger continued to simmer inside T.J. Eventually, he thought, I'll get away from this guy. When I do, I should have as much information as I can to give the police so they'll be able to find him.

"Where do you live?" T.J. asked.

"Nowhere. I told you—they burned my store."

"You lived at the store?"

"I had an apartment over the store. Best commute in town."

So he had lost his home as well as his business. T.J. didn't blame Brody for being upset. Still, going on an arson rampage wasn't going to help.

"Where do you stay now? Where did you sleep last night?"

"Where you found me."

"You slept in the Crowleys' barn last night?"

"Nobody was using that old barn and I only stayed there one night."

In other words, T.J. thought, he doesn't have a regular

home. He sleeps in barns or abandoned buildings. It will be hard to find Brody again, once I get away from him.

"Where do you get money?" T.J. asked. "You have to buy food, and gas for your truck."

"I use my paycheck."

"You have a job?" That was a surprise.

"Sometimes."

"Where do you work?"

"Here and there. When I need money, I go to a state employment office."

That would help. The cops could alert the employment office to watch for Brody.

"They have jobs for a couple of days," Brody added.

"Temporary work," T.J. said.

"It's better than robbing a bank."

T.J. looked at Brody to see if he was serious. Brody gazed straight ahead at the road.

"How many fires have you started?" T.J. asked.

"I don't keep track."

"You must have some idea. Five? Ten?"

Brody shrugged.

"Did you burn down the tractor shed on Ridge Road yesterday?"

Brody shrugged again.

"Have you started fires in other places, or just around here?"

"None of your business."

T.J. couldn't think of anything else to ask.

———

"Dane! Telephone!" His sister sounded annoyed as she yelled down the stairs. No doubt she had hoped it was her boyfriend calling.

Dane looked at the clock. Who would call him this late? He turned down the sound on the TV and picked up the phone.

"Dane, this is Ted Stenson, T.J.'s father. Is T.J. at your house?"

"No."

"Do you know where he is?"

"I thought he was home. He told me he was going to watch *Top Gun* and it's still on."

"He isn't here and neither is his grandmother. We're a bit concerned. When did you talk to him last?"

"A little after seven. I called to remind him that *Top Gun* was on and he said he was planning to watch it."

"Did he say anything else?"

Dane thought for a moment. "No. We didn't talk long. I tried to call again later, during a commercial, but no one answered."

"What time was that?"

"About nine-thirty, I think."

"Thanks, Dane. If you hear from T.J., call me right away."

Dane promised that he would. After he hung up, Dane remembered the one other thing T.J. had said—that he was going to go feed the neighbors' pets. Dane hesitated. Should he call Mr. Stenson back and tell him that? T.J. had been taking care of the Crowleys' animals all week; it wouldn't be news to Mr. Stenson.

Dane decided not to call.

Grandma Ruth shifted from side to side. It was cold on the ground and her back ached. Tired as she was, she was too uncomfortable to fall asleep.

She wished David would come.

Perhaps she shouldn't wait for him, after all. Perhaps she should walk on and find her own way home.

Grandma Ruth stood up, clutching her purse. She had better hurry. Amelia and Marion would be coming home from school soon and Grandma Ruth liked to be there, waiting, when her daughters got home.

The winding country road passed farms periodically, but the buildings were always set back off the road. No one saw them drive by; there was no opportunity for T.J. to call for help.

"Where are we going?" T.J. asked.

"I don't know. I never know until I get there."

"In other words, we are driving aimlessly around looking for a building for you to torch."

T.J. wished he knew for sure if Brody had a gun. *Wishing won't help. Take action.*

He looked at Brody; Brody had both hands on the steering wheel. The pocket of his jacket seemed flat—too flat to contain a gun. Had the bulge T.J. feared earlier been merely Brody's fist?

T.J.'s hand shot out and reached for Brody's pocket.

"Hey!" Brody's hand came down quickly, shoving T.J. away. "What do you think you're doing?"

"What do you have in your pocket?" T.J. asked.

"It's mine."

"I know it's yours. I just wondered what it is."

Brody kept his left hand on the wheel and put his right hand protectively over the pocket. "It's been with me on every revenge," he said. "Never failed me once."

"What about the shed you just burned, the one with the pony? Did you use what's in your pocket then?"

"Sure I did. What else would I use?"

It wasn't a gun, then. Brody had not fired a gun back at the pony shed.

"Could I see it? If I promise not to touch, would you show it to me?"

Brody hesitated for only a second. Then, like a proud new parent displaying a photo of the baby, he pulled a cigarette lighter out of his pocket. Cradling the lighter in the palm of his hand, he held it out for T.J. to admire.

T.J. stared. A lousy cigarette lighter! I've been terrified that he was going to shoot me and all he has in his pocket is a crummy lighter.

"It's all I have left of him." Brody's voice was low; the hysterical edge was gone.

"Who?"

"My old man. He died last year, a couple of weeks after I took over the store."

"I'm sorry."

"That store was my old man's whole life and it was gone in twenty minutes." Brody slammed his fist against the steering wheel. "The fire department never came. The cops never came. Nobody helped me."

"I'm sorry," T.J. repeated, and he meant it. It must have been horrible.

"Every time I set a fire, I do it for him, to make up for losing

88

his store. I'm going to make people realize what it's like to lose everything and not get any help." Brody's voice dropped and T.J. had to lean toward him to hear. "That was the worst part," Brody said. "I shouted and shouted for help and nobody came."

They rode on in silence.

The next time we stop, T.J. thought, I'll make my break. Next time, I'll get away. I could probably have done it before, if I had known he only had a cigarette lighter in his pocket, rather than a Saturday night special.

"Twenty-three," Brody said.

"What?"

"Twenty-three. I've had revenge twenty-three times."

Twenty-three fires! T.J. wondered if that was true or if Brody was exaggerating. If the number was anywhere near that many, it was amazing that he was still free.

"You're lucky you haven't been caught."

"It isn't luck. I'm smart. I pick places where it isn't easy to get help. That's the point, you know. And I keep moving."

His luck can't hold out forever, T.J. thought. Sooner or later, he will be caught, and I hope it's sooner.

*Take action, T.J. Make it happen.*

T.J. closed his eyes and planned exactly how to make his move. He visualized himself getting out of the truck and running into a gas station. He wouldn't say anything about a bank robber this time. He needed a story that would be believed instantly by the person who heard it, something that would make the person call for help immediately.

In his imagination, he heard himself cry, "I'm sick. I'm going to pass out. Call 9-1-1." Then he would collapse on the floor. That ought to get help quickly.

# Chapter Nine

Craig Ackerley could hardly believe his good fortune. First, his parents called from the Open House at school to say they were going out for coffee and would be late getting home, and then his brother, Ben, decided to go to the eleven o'clock movie.

Craig pretended to be watching television. He waved absentmindedly when Ben said he was leaving. As soon as the door closed behind Ben, Craig switched off the television and got to his feet. He peered out the window as Ben sprinted down the front sidewalk and climbed into his friend's waiting car.

When the car drove off, Craig hurried to Ben's bedroom and opened the closet. After pushing Ben's clothes aside, he reached into the far corner for Ben's suitcase. He dragged it out of the closet, opened it, and removed a can of beer.

Craig popped open the can and drank it as quickly as he

could. Belching loudly, he opened a second can and drank it, too. It didn't taste as good as he remembered from the times when Ben took him along with his friends to a drinking party. The beer would be better if it was cold and it wasn't as much fun to drink alone.

I need a drinking buddy, Craig decided. I need somebody to party with for an hour or two. He removed two six-packs from the suitcase before he closed it and shoved it back where he had found it.

Craig closed his bedroom door, so his parents would think he was asleep when they got home. Tucking a six-pack under each arm, he stepped out into the night and walked rapidly away from home.

His first stop was just down the street, at Lyle's house. Lyle's parents might have stayed late at the Open House, too, and Lyle had confided to Craig that he sometimes had a small glass of his mother's wine when he was home alone. Lyle would make a fine drinking buddy.

As Craig knocked on Lyle's door, he saw his parents' car turn into his own driveway. It's my lucky night, he thought. I got out just in time.

Lyle answered the door.

"Party time," Craig said. "Down in the woods."

Lyle hesitated. "My folks went to that meeting at school," he said, "but they'll be home any minute. I thought they'd be here before this."

"All the parents went out to eat."

"Are you sure?"

"Positive." Craig hiccuped. "Leave them a note. Say you're at my house, doing homework. But hurry."

Lyle grinned. "I'll be out in a second," he said.

"Bring your mother's wine," Craig said.

A minute later, the two boys headed down the sidewalk. Lyle walked quickly, nervous that a car would pass and the driver would recognize him and see what he was carrying.

"We should have put this stuff in a brown paper bag," he said. "Then it would look as if we were carrying groceries home."

"Quit worrying," Craig said. "Who's going to see us?"

They approached a newly built home, the last to be constructed in the Forest View Estates subdivision where they lived. "Those two new guys on the basketball team live here," Lyle said.

"The brothers? Allen and Nicholas?"

"Right. They moved in a couple of weeks ago."

Craig hiccuped again.

Lyle laughed. "I think you started the party before you got to my house," he said.

"Let's see if Allen and Nicholas want to go with us."

Lyle stopped. "I don't know them very well," he said. "What if they blab? What if their parents answer the door?"

"They won't blab, if they know what's good for them. And if an adult answers the door, we'll pretend we have the wrong address. I'll ask for directions to my house." Craig laughed loudly at that idea as he marched up the sidewalk of the new house and rang the doorbell.

Lyle trailed after him, ready to run. He was relieved when Nicholas answered the door.

"Get your brother," Craig said. "We're having a party."

"Now?" Nicholas said. "It's kind of late."

92

"It's a surprise party. You're supposed to come as you are."

Allen joined his brother at the door. "What's going on?" he asked.

"We're invited to a party," Nicholas said. "Do you think Mom and Dad would let us go?"

"Your parents aren't home?" Lyle said.

"Dad's out of town. Mom's home but she's already asleep."

"She starts her new job tomorrow," Allen added. "I don't think we should wake her up."

"The whole basketball team is coming to the party," Craig said. "It's a tradition, on the night before the first game."

"It is?" Lyle said.

"If your mother's asleep," Craig said, "you can come to the party and get back again and she'll never know you left."

Allen and Nicholas looked at each other. "We could leave a note," Allen said, "in case she wakes up."

Nicholas nodded. "We'll be right out."

Craig bounded back down the sidewalk, grinning widely.

"You nerd," Lyle said. "Why did you say the whole team is coming? They'll see right away that it's only us."

"By then they'll be having such a good time, they'll want to stay. This is going to be a great party."

Allen and Nicholas came out of the house and joined them. Allen carried a camping lantern. "I couldn't find a flashlight," he explained, "and I like to see where I'm going."

"Turn that thing off," Lyle said. "We're trying not to get noticed."

Allen switched off the lantern. "Where is the party going to be?" he asked.

Lyle looked at Craig. "Where are we going?" he asked.

"I know the perfect place," Craig said. "It's a big old willow tree on the edge of the swamp. My brother and his buddies go there all the time."

"The party isn't at someone's house?" Nicholas said.

"What's the matter?" Craig said. "You chicken to go into the woods at night?"

"No. It's just that . . ."

*"Cluck, cluck, cluck,"* said Craig.

"I'm not scared," Nicholas said. "I thought we were going to someone's house, that's all."

"Don't think so much," Craig said. "Thinking gets you in trouble."

"Where are the rest of the guys?" Allen asked.

"They're meeting us at the willow tree," Craig said.

"Oh, man," Lyle said. "I can't believe you sometimes."

"Are you *sure* the whole team is doing this?" Nicholas said.

"Come on," Craig said. "Let's move it." He took off, running toward the end of the street, where the swampy area began.

Lyle ran after him.

Allen and Nicholas hesitated, looked at each other, and shrugged. Then they ran, too, their tennis shoes landing rhythmically on the pavement. They followed Craig past the last of the Forest View Estates houses, toward the weeping willow at the edge of the swamp.

Grandma Ruth sat on a fallen log. Sweat trickled down the back of her neck. Somehow, she had lost the path again. Or had there ever been a path? She wasn't sure.

Her back ached and she felt as if she had been walking for

a week. No matter which way she turned, the woods were the same.

Once, an hour or so ago, she had come out of the woods near that odd church where David and the preacher had told her to stay and sing hymns but she did not go inside. She had not liked that church and she needed to get home. Quickly, she had turned away and headed into the woods again, struggling through the tangle of undergrowth that grabbed at her ankles and snagged her skirt. Her cheeks stung from scratches where branches had brushed her face. Maybe if she sat on this old log and rested, David would come looking for her.

She wiped her brow with the back of her hand. Whatever had possessed her to go off berry picking in the middle of the night? David always said she didn't have the sense of a hound dog's fleas, and this time it seemed he was right.

A chorus of frogs sang loudly. She looked around, trying to figure out where she was, but she saw only dark trees, twisted and menacing.

A mosquito buzzed in her ear and she brushed it away. Another bit her on the arm. She would have to keep moving. If she sat here, the mosquitoes would have her for dinner.

Wearily, she stood up. The frogs sang an encore.

Frogs. Frogs and mosquitoes. She must be near a swampy area, for the mosquitoes to be this thick and the frogs to be so loud.

A swamp. Didn't she and David used to take a picnic across the swamp, to a big willow tree? Or was it T.J.? One of them. One of them used to go with her, balancing carefully as they walked across the fallen trees that made a path across the swamp. They would eat their lunch hidden in the circle of the willow tree's loving arms.

Grandma Ruth remembered how safe and snug she had felt there. How happy. Maybe she could find that tree. Maybe T.J. was there now, with the sandwiches and oranges, waiting for her.

She licked her lips at the thought of an orange. Her mouth was so dry. A sweet, juicy orange would taste wonderful right now.

Come to think of it, T.J. had said something about waiting for him. Hadn't he? "Wait right there," he had said. "Don't leave."

Grandma Ruth tried to walk faster. When the ground became muddier, with less growth, her shoes sank in the muck. Her legs ached with the effort but she was determined to keep going.

Yes, she thought, I'm almost to the swamp. I'll be able to find the willow tree and T.J. will be there and he'll give me something to drink and help me find my way home.

When she emerged from the last of the woods, she stopped and smiled. She recognized this place. Moonlight lit the fallen logs, making them look like alligators resting in the mud.

Grandma Ruth stepped carefully onto the first log and, tucking her purse under her chin, put her arms out sideways, to keep her balance. Slowly and deliberately, she moved across the logs. When she came to the place where the log path turned left, she stopped and looked up.

Ahead of her, the willow tree glowed with light. All night long, the trees in the woods had seemed black and dangerous, their dark leafy fingers linked together to bar her way. But the willow looked green and welcoming. She saw a cascade of individual branches, each covered with bright green leaves that trailed their tips on the ground. The light came from inside the branches, from the area near the trunk.

A loud cackle of laughter jarred the night. The frogs stopped singing. Grandma Ruth stood still, blinking in surprise. The laughter came again, even louder. It was two voices this time. Grandma Ruth's heart beat faster with relief and glad anticipation. She had been right. David—or was it T.J.?—was waiting for her at the willow tree. Maybe they were both there, and Edward, too. Edward. Oh, she hoped dear Edward was with them. It had been such a long time since she had seen her husband.

Happily, she stepped off the last log and approached the long, sweeping branches of the huge old willow.

The truck stopped.

Startled, T.J. opened his eyes and looked out. They were parked beside a long row of old sheds, all connected. A faded sign on the roof said, "Langley's Chicken Ranch." A newer sign in front of the buildings said, STORAGE SPACE FOR RENT CHEAP.

These buildings were larger than the pony shed had been. They had once been painted red but the small amount of paint that was left was faded and chipped, making them look untidy, like a molting chicken. Still, they were sturdy, with solid walls and a decent roof. Padlocks hung from each of the doors.

T.J.'s spirits sank. He had been visualizing exactly what he would do and say when Brody stopped for gas. Instead, Brody had stopped where there were no people.

"Make sure it's empty this time," T.J. said.

Brody motioned for T.J. to be quiet. He got out and walked toward the row of sheds.

Quickly, T.J. got out, too. He didn't trust Brody to look inside the sheds before he set them ablaze and he did not want to dash into a burning building and rescue any more animals. If there were any living creatures in these sheds, T.J. planned to turn them loose right now, before Brody got his lighter out.

Brody cupped his hands on the sides of his face and looked through the dirty window of the first shed. "Oh, man," he said. "We've hit the jackpot."

T.J. looked in, too, and saw an elegant old car. T.J. couldn't tell in the dark what kind it was but from the size and shape he guessed an early Model T or some other classic car.

Brody went from shed to shed, pulling on the padlocks. T.J. knew he was hoping one of them wasn't clicked tightly into place.

T.J. went to the second shed and looked in the window. This one contained a large boat, on a boat trailer.

At the fifth shed, Brody said, "Bingo," and removed the lock. Then he continued down the row, pulling on the rest of the padlocks.

T.J. slid open the unlocked shed door. He felt along the wall beside the door, found a light switch, and pushed it. As the light flickered on, he stared in surprise. The shed was jammed full—not with live animals, but with wooden ones.

"Look at this," T.J. said. "There are parts of an old merry-go-round stored in here."

There were carved horses, chariots, an ostrich—even a

wooden pig with a fancy carved saddle. Like the outside of the shed, their paint was faded and chipped but enough color remained to give the overall appearance of red, blue, gold, and green. "This must have been in a circus or an amusement park," T.J. said.

Brody looked in the door.

"You can't set a fire here," T.J. said. "That old car in the first shed is worth a bundle and these are antiques. They're works of art."

"Tough."

"Old carousels like this are worth a lot of money."

"They are?"

"Absolutely. Collectors pay thousands of dollars for just one old merry-go-round horse and there must be two dozen of them in here. This place is worth a fortune."

Brody peered at the carved animals. "They look old and worn out to me."

"The older they are, the more they're worth. Look," he said, pointing to his left, "there's the calliope or organ or whatever it's called that was in the center of the merry-go-round. It's what played the music. I wonder if it still works."

"How do you know so much about old merry-go-rounds?"

"My grandmother was interested in antiques. She used to take me to antique shows with her. When I was little and we saw carousel horses displayed, I always wanted to buy one but Grandma Ruth said they were too expensive."

"How much do you think all this is worth?"

T.J. did a quick mental count. "There must be twenty carved animals, plus the organ and all the other parts. As a rough guess, I'd say at least one hundred thousand dollars."

T.J. could tell that Brody was impressed. "We'd be fools to burn this shed," T.J. continued, "without taking this stuff out of here first."

"You mean, you want to steal it?"

"I doubt the owner would give permission for us to take it."

"I don't know. I never stole anything."

"You could buy a lot of gasoline for one hundred thousand dollars. You wouldn't ever have to do temporary work again."

Brody scratched his head. "One hundred thousand smack-eroos." He slapped his hands together, as if he'd made a momentous decision. "We'll load this stuff in the truck and take it to Seattle and sell it."

"Good plan." Excellent plan, in fact, T.J. thought. Any reputable antique dealer would ask questions about how Brody happened to own such treasures. They'd want to know the background of the carousel and where Brody got the animals. If the police hadn't found T.J. in the meantime, Brody was almost certain to attract their attention when he tried to sell the old carousel animals.

"Turn that light off," Brody said, and then did it himself.

The horses were heavy. Brody and T.J. each carried one to the truck. Partway there, T.J. had to put his down and rest.

"They aren't all going to fit," Brody said.

"No. After we sell the first load, we'll need to make another trip." The more the better, T.J. thought. Maybe someone will notice that some of the animals are missing. Maybe the cops will be waiting for us to come back for the rest.

"We need blankets or something, to protect them," T.J. said, when he had his horse on the ground beside the truck.

"We can't just pile them in the back of the truck. They'll get scratched."

"We can use the tarp."

"That will do for one or two animals. We'll need something else to protect the others."

Brody lifted the tarp and stopped. He looked at the cans of gasoline. He slipped his hand in his pocket and removed the cigarette lighter. He stood beside the truck, turning the lighter over and over in his palm. With his other hand, he picked up the end gasoline can, the one he took with him to the pony shed, and lifted it out of the truck.

T.J. climbed into the back of the truck and reached for the tarp. He spread it on the bed of the truck. "We can lay two horses on this tarp and then wrap the tarp over the top of the horses, to protect them," he said.

There was no answer.

T.J. turned to look at Brody. He was walking toward the storage sheds, carrying the can of gasoline.

"Wait!" T.J. yelled.

He jumped off the truck and ran after Brody. He grabbed Brody's sleeve. "We have to get the carousel animals out first," he said.

"No," Brody said. "This is my chance for the perfect revenge." His eyes had a glazed look. He pushed T.J.'s hand away and strode into the shed that held the carousel animals. He began pouring the gasoline around the inside of the shed.

"What about the money?" T.J. said. "We can't sell the animals if you burn them. You might just as well set fire to a stack of one hundred dollar bills."

Brody appeared not to hear or see T.J. Once he had the

can of gasoline in his hand, his mind seemed to block out everything else. Slowly and methodically, he trickled gasoline around the inside of the shed.

"You can't do this," T.J. said. "Not with the carousel animals still inside."

But even as he said the words, he knew Brody would do it. If it didn't bother him to set fire to a building that contained a live pony, it certainly wasn't going to bother him to burn a collection of old wooden animals.

T.J. rushed into the shed and dragged the wooden pig out through the door. He pulled it across the ground until it was far enough from the shed that it should be safe. He started back to get another animal and then stopped just inside the door.

Brody was on the far side of the shed now, bent over. It was too dark for T.J. to see for sure what Brody was doing but undoubtedly he was trickling the gasoline along the base of the wall. At any rate, he wasn't paying any attention to T.J.

T.J. hesitated for only an instant. He was tempted to keep dragging the animals out, trying to remove as many as he could. If he worked fast, he could probably remove most of them before the fire got too bad. He should try to save the unusual ones, anyway—the ostrich and the sea horse and the organ. Besides being valuable, they were beautiful.

Instead of reaching for another animal, he backed away from Brody, stepped away from the shed and ran.

# Chapter Ten

Dane left the TV on when *Top Gun* ended. The news was on next and he wanted to know if the Seattle Seahawks had decided who would start as quarterback on Sunday. Since the sports news was usually last, Dane went out to the kitchen and got a bag of peanuts. When he came back, the announcers were finishing a story about a bank robbery and murder. Dane was glad to hear the murderer was already in custody.

He took a handful of peanuts and began to shell them. He had just popped the first peanut into his mouth when his attention was yanked back to the news broadcast.

"An elderly Pine Ridge woman and her grandson are missing tonight," the announcer said, "and search parties are organizing to look for them. The woman has Alzheimer's disease and is easily confused. If anyone has information or knows the whereabouts of Ruth Windham and her grandson, T.J. Stenson, please call the sheriff's office immediately."

Dane dropped the peanuts and bolted upstairs to where his parents were just getting into bed. "T.J.'s missing!" he cried. "He and his grandma are gone. They just announced it on television."

"Missing?" Dane's mother asked. "What happened?"

"I don't know. Mr. Stenson called me just before you got home from the Open House, to see if I knew where T.J. was, and I said I thought he was home watching *Top Gun*. He wanted to know when I last talked to T.J. and what he had said. I told him, and then Mr. Stenson just said, 'Thanks,' and hung up. Now T.J.'s name was on the news and the police are organizing a search party and I have to go over there and help."

Dane's father reached for the telephone. "What's T.J.'s number?" he asked. Dane gave it and his father dialed. Someone answered on the first ring.

Dane listened impatiently to his father's end of the conversation.

His father hung up and said, "They're both gone, with no clue as to what happened." He began dressing as he talked. "Ted Stenson thinks maybe the grandmother wandered away and T.J. went out looking for her. I'll go with you, Dane."

Dane's mother said, "Wait for me," and grabbed some jeans and a sweatshirt from her closet. "I'll wake up Susan and tell her where we're going."

When Dane's older sister heard what was happening, she said she would help, too. Ten minutes later Dane's whole family was in their car, headed toward the Stenson home.

"If that poor woman is lost," Dane's mother said, "she

must be terrified. Amelia Stenson told me her mother is like a young child most of the time."

"T.J.'s grandmother wears an identification bracelet," Dane said, "with her name, address, and phone number on it. T.J. told me they got it for her just in case she ever wandered away and got lost."

"An ID bracelet only helps if someone finds her," his father said.


T.J. sprinted past the truck. The sheds wouldn't be out in the middle of nowhere. They used to be part of a chicken ranch, so there had to be a house nearby. Maybe he would get to act out the scene he had visualized, after all. Instead of doing it at a gas station, he would do it at a farmhouse.

The ground was uneven, as if no vehicle drove regularly across it. He hoped the house, if he found one, was occupied.

His foot hit a shallow hole and he fell to his knees, twisting his left ankle. He got up, rubbed at the ankle, and limped on.

As he ran, he rethought his plan. Maybe he shouldn't pretend to be sick. He was sure it would work, but if someone in the house believed he was ill, they would call for an ambulance, and medics would not be equipped to put out the fire. Ambulance attendants would have been fine if he and Brody were at a gas station, where there was no fire involved. Here, there was the fire to consider. At least three of those sheds contained valuable merchandise; probably the others did, too.

T.J. hoped that a fire truck might arrive in time to save the carousel animals and the old car and the boat. He decided to tell the truth.

He saw the outline of a house ahead: a two-story farmhouse, with a wide porch across the front. The house was dark but he could tell there were curtains in the windows and a bicycle leaned against the porch rail.

He took the porch steps two at a time, and pounded on the door of the house. He tried to turn the knob, but the door was locked. A light went on in one of the upstairs windows. He pounded again.

The outside porch light came on. The door opened a crack. T.J. saw a chain lock and, behind it, a woman's face.

"Call the fire department," T.J. said. "Call the police! I need help."

"Who are you?"

"There's a man with me, an arsonist. He made me go with him. I need help. Please let me in. Please!"

"If you need help," the woman said, "I will call the police for you. But I can't let you in my house."

"He's setting fire to your storage sheds," T.J. said. "He's pouring gasoline around the one with all the carousel animals in it."

The woman's face disappeared from the other side of the door. He saw the curtains open on the side of the house toward the sheds. The woman looked out.

T.J. put his fingers through the crack in the door and tried to unhook the chain lock.

The woman screamed, "Fire!"

T.J. spun around and looked behind him. The shed had erupted in flames.

T.J. could hear the woman calling for help. Her voice was

106

frantic, giving directions, pleading with the fire fighters to hurry.

When she hung up, she ran back to the door, undid the chain and opened the door. As she rushed past T.J., she said, "There are some buckets on the back porch. Fill them with water! Hurry!" She turned on an outside faucet on the side of the house, filled a tin watering can, and ran toward the sheds with her pink bathrobe flapping around her knees.

The flames leaped and danced, lighting the sky. T.J. could smell the smoke already. He knew it would take far more than a watering can and a couple of buckets to put out such a blaze.

I should go with her, T.J. thought. Maybe I could still drag those beautiful old carved animals out of the shed before they're destroyed.

He looked across the pasture toward the burning shed. He didn't move. If he went back there, chances were good that Brody would try to grab him again. Even without a gun, T.J. knew Brody would not hesitate to use force, if necessary, to keep T.J. with him. Or Brody would lie again, convincing the woman that T.J. had set the fire or that T.J. was Brody's son who had run away from home.

If he went to help the woman, he could find himself back in the truck long before help arrived, heading down the road for more revenge.

Much as he hated to think of the old merry-go-round animals going up in smoke, trying to save them wasn't worth the risk. T.J. had been willing to jeopardize his own safety to save the frightened pony. The pony was a living creature. But the carousel horses, valuable as they might be, were merely things. Compared to his safety, they were worth nothing.

The woman did not return for more water. The door to the house stood wide open. Feeling like a burglar, T.J. entered and closed the door behind him. He slipped the chain lock into place, making certain that Brody couldn't follow him into the house.

A small mirror hung beside the door. When he saw his reflection, he could see why the woman had been afraid to let him in her house. His face was streaked with soot, there were bits of ash in his hair, and his sweatshirt was filthy. He looked like he had not had a bath in a month.

He heard no voices or any other sign that anyone was in the house with him. Surely, if someone else was here, they would have heard the woman calling for help.

T.J. turned and looked to his left; the large living room was empty. T.J. walked to his right, through the dining area and into the kitchen. He turned on the kitchen light and glanced quickly around, hoping to see a telephone.

He heard sirens in the distance, wailing like wolves at the full moon. He returned to the dining room. From that window, he saw the red lights of the fire engine approach. The engine slowed and turned in the driveway. The sky glowed with the white moonlight and the yellow flames and the circling red lights.

T.J. leaned on the windowsill and watched. His bones ached and his head throbbed. He wondered how long he had been gone. It seemed like a month since he and Grandma Ruth had started across the pasture to feed the Crowleys' animals. Remembering how cross he had been, how he had tried to hurry her by saying David was dead, T.J. felt ashamed. She can't help being the way she is.

He wondered how long Grandma Ruth had sat on the bale of hay in the Crowleys' barn, singing hymns. She no longer had any sense of time. If nobody came to get her, she might sit there all night, singing, "Holy, Holy, Holy." Maybe she was *still* there.

T.J. heard shouting outside. He watched as the fire fighters jumped off the truck, unrolled long canvas hoses, and began battling the blaze.

Where was Brody? T.J. looked to the side of the barn, where the truck had been parked. He saw only the carousel pig that he had dragged away from the shed. The moon shone down on the empty road.

Cautiously, he went down the hall, looked into a bedroom, and saw that no one was in it. He heard more sirens. He went in the bedroom and crossed to the window on the side of the house toward the sheds. Another fire truck arrived and two police cars.

It would be safe to go out there now. With all those fire fighters and police on the scene, T.J. would finally get help. Even if Brody was still around, hiding and watching the fire, he wouldn't dare try to grab T.J.

It's over, T.J. thought. I got away from him.

He turned to leave the bedroom. As he did, he saw a small bedside table. On it stood a telephone.

He sat on the edge of the bed and dialed.

He got a recording. "You must first dial a one and the area code," the recording said. He tried again, this time adding the one and the area code before he dialed his own number.

His father answered on the first ring. "Where are you?" he cried, when he heard T.J.'s voice. "Are you all right? What happened?"

Quickly, T.J. explained how he had stumbled upon a man hiding in the Crowleys' barn and he thought it was the bank robber and the man made T.J. go with him. "You need to go over to Crowleys' right away, Dad," he said. "I left . . ."

"We've already been there. Where are you, T.J.? Where are you calling from?"

"I don't know," he said. He explained about the fires. "I'm going to talk to the police now. I'll call you back when I find out where I am."

"No! Don't hang up. Look around. See if you can find something with an address on it."

T.J. put the phone on the bed and walked to a small desk. Inside were greeting cards, a checkbook, and a stack of bills addressed to Mrs. Jane Langley.

He read the address to his dad, relieved that he wasn't as far from home as he had feared.

"Sit tight," his dad said. "We've already reported that you were missing. I'll let the police know we've located you and then we'll be there to pick you up."

"Hurry."

"We will. Can you give me a phone number where you are?"

T.J. read the number that was taped to the front of the telephone.

"Good. In case we have trouble finding the address, I'll know how to reach you. Meanwhile, you go talk to the fire fighters or the sheriff or whatever officials are on the scene.

Tell them who you are and how you got there. Stay with them until we arrive."

"I will."

"And keep Grandma Ruth with you."

"What?"

"Keep her close. We don't want to take a chance that the arsonist would come back after you and somehow manage to take her hostage by herself. Or she could wander off and get lost in a strange area."

"She isn't here."

"Where is she? You didn't leave her alone with that lunatic, did you?"

"She never went in the truck with us. I left her in the Crowleys' barn. I told her it was a church."

There was silence on the other end of the line.

"Did you hear me, Dad?"

"Hold on a minute, T.J."

T.J. heard his dad telling someone else that Grandma Ruth was not with T.J. Then his dad said, "I won't be able to come after you right away. The police need my help here. We're going to start a search for her."

"She's in the Crowleys' barn. I told Grandma Ruth that the barn was a church and she was in charge of the hymns and she should stay there until the preacher came. I thought you would have found her by now."

"She isn't there," Mr. Stenson said.

"You've been to the barn?"

"That's the first place we looked for you. We called Dane as soon as we realized you weren't home. When he didn't know where you were, we called Crowleys and when no one answered we went over there. We couldn't think where else you would go without leaving a note. No one came to the door and we saw the dogs were loose in the field so we put them back in their pen and then . . ."

"Did you see my message?"

"What message?"

"I scratched a message in the dirt next to the dog pen."

"I didn't see it. It was dark and just as I put the dogs in the pen, I heard your mother yelling for me. She'd gone in the barn and found Grandma Ruth's hat on the floor."

"Oh."

"We thought Grandma Ruth was with you."

"No." There was such a lump in his throat that he could barely say the word. "No, she isn't with me. I don't know where she is."

"What time did you leave her in the barn?"

"About seven-thirty. What time is it now?"

"Nearly eleven-thirty."

Eleven-thirty. It was four hours since he'd left Grandma Ruth alone in the barn. Four long hours. If she had left the barn right away, she could be anywhere by now.

"I have to go," Mr. Stenson said. "Your mother's frantic and the police are asking dozens of questions. We'll be there as soon as we can."

T.J. hung up. He looked out the window again and saw that the fire was out. He wondered if they had saved any of the carousel animals. He wondered if Brody got away or whether the police had him. Most of all, he wondered what had happened to Grandma Ruth.

# Chapter Eleven

T.J. still heard no noise from inside the house. Apparently, the woman lived here alone.

He opened the front door cautiously and looked out. In the distance, the red lights of the fire engines whirled around and around. There were flashing blue lights, too, belonging to the two police cars. The effect was circuslike, which T.J. thought was ironic since the fire had probably ruined the old carousel forever.

He did not see Brody's truck. He left the house and sprinted toward the flashing lights, keeping a sharp eye out in case Brody was parked behind the house or somewhere else that T.J. didn't see him. He didn't want the blue truck to rush at him in the dark and have Brody swoop him away, like a hawk catching a sparrow.

Ahead, he saw the woman and a man in uniform, standing a ways off from the fire fighters. T.J. ran toward them.

As soon as the woman saw him, she pointed her finger at him and shouted, "That's him! That's the boy who started the fire!"

Immediately, two officers approached T.J.

"I didn't start it," T.J. said.

"He pounded on my door and woke me up and told me the sheds were burning. He probably robbed me while I was out here throwing water on the blaze. That's how these people operate, you know. They trick you into unlocking your door and then when you do, they . . ."

"Please, Mrs. Langley," one of the officers said. "We'll handle this, if you don't mind."

"That beautiful merry-go-round is ruined," the woman said. "All those wonderful animals." She began to cry. "And the other units are damaged, too. I'll lose all my renters."

"What's your name?" the officer asked T.J.

"T.J. Stenson. The arsonist is named Brody; he kidnapped me. I thought he had a gun and when he told me to go with him, I did. My parents have already reported that I'm missing."

"Check it out," the first officer said and the second officer went to the patrol car.

T.J. briefly told what had happened, starting with when he opened the Crowleys' barn door and discovered Brody inside.

The second officer returned. "He's telling the truth," he said. "His parents called the King County sheriff an hour ago."

At last, T.J. thought, someone believes me.

The police questioned him about Brody and T.J. tried to remember as many details as possible. When he described

Brody's earring, one of the officers exclaimed, "I've seen him! He was at a fire a few days ago. I even talked to him when we suspected arson, but I decided he was just a spark."

"A what?" T.J. asked.

"A spark. That's what we call people who like to hang around and watch fires whenever they can. They're usually harmless—just fans who like to see the action."

"Fans?" T.J. said. "You mean, like basketball fans?"

"You got it. Some sparks even listen to the police radio in order to know when there's a fire to chase. It's a hobby with them."

What a weird hobby, T.J. thought.

The officer shook his head. "Usually I can tell a genuine spark," he said, "but that one had me fooled. He kept talking about his old man being proud of him; I thought his father used to be a fire fighter."

The officers asked more questions. When T.J. told about Brody's revenge, the police looked at each other and rolled their eyes.

"Great," one of them said. "Just what we need, a pyro-maniac who thinks more fires will make up for his own loss."

"Part of the time, he seemed perfectly normal," T.J. said. "He only got weird when he was talking about his fires."

"Grief does strange things to people. So does anger. Or maybe he's always only had one oar in the water."

"I saw one other case," another officer said, "where it turned out the guy had a chemical imbalance. Half the time he was as sane as I am and then, other times, it was like he stepped over some invisible line and became a whole different person."

"Let's get a bulletin out on him," the other officer replied. "He can't be too far away."

The officers had CB radios and cellular phones in their patrol cars. After a brief telephone conversation, one of the officers, Sergeant Donnell, told T.J. that he would drive him home. "Your parents can't come to get you because they're helping the sheriff organize a search for your grandmother," Sergeant Donnell said, "but I'll have you home in less than half an hour."

T.J.'s fatigue vanished. That was definitely the best news he'd heard all night.

During the ride home, T.J. told the sergeant every detail of his time with Brody. When he got to the part about the pony, Sergeant Donnell said, "You're a brave kid."

"Me?" T.J. said. "I'm not brave at all. I was scared silly but I couldn't let the pony burn to death."

"That's what being brave is," Sergeant Donnell replied. "It's acting on your convictions. People always think police officers are brave; they think we aren't afraid of anything. Well, the truth is, we get just as scared as the next guy but we're willing to act on our convictions. I'll take a risk in order to prevent a crime. You took a risk in order to save the pony."

That's true, T.J. thought. Maybe I *am* brave, when there is something worth taking a risk for. Maybe I'm not such a wimp as Craig Ackerley thinks I am.

Just then, the police radio announced, "This is Car Eighteen. We've spotted an old blue pickup heading west on I-90 near Issaquah. The driver appears to be alone."

"That's him," T.J. said. "That's Brody."

The radio gave a location and a second voice broke in to

say that Car Twenty would be there in two minutes, for backup.

Less than five minutes later, T.J. heard the report: "Suspect is in custody. He appears mentally unstable. He admits setting the fire and keeps saying his old man would be proud of him. We're taking him in for a psychiatric evaluation."

"It seems Brody lost more than his store," Sergeant Donnell said. "He also lost his mental competence. His twisted mind now justifies arson, the same crime that caused his troubles."

The patrol car left the freeway. "Many people face terrible tragedies," Sergeant Donnell continued, "but they emerge stronger and more determined to make something good of their lives. While Brody had a valid reason for being angry and sad, he allowed the fire and the loss of his father's store to destroy the rest of his own life, too. What a waste."

When they arrived at T.J.'s house, Sergeant Donnell had to park half a block away. There were two police cars in the Stensons' driveway, and half a dozen other cars were parked along the street.

The yard lights blazed and every light in the house seemed to be on. Through the living room window, T.J. saw a group of about thirty people. The babble of voices carried across the lawn.

If Grandma Ruth did find her way home, T.J. thought, she would be too intimidated by all the people and noise to go inside. They couldn't even take her to a shopping mall anymore. Crowds of chattering people made her fearful, probably because she didn't understand who they were or what they were saying.

Sergeant Donnell followed T.J. to the door. When the people

inside saw T.J., everyone cheered. Flashbulbs popped; a reporter started asking questions.

Mrs. Stenson ran to him and hugged him. Her eyes were red and her makeup was streaked. "Thank goodness you're safe," she said. She turned to Sergeant Donnell. "Thank you for bringing him home," she said.

"Have you found Grandma Ruth?" T.J. asked.

Mrs. Stenson shook her head. Tears spilled onto her cheeks and she wiped them with the back of one hand. "The searchers are getting ready to leave now. Dad and a sheriff's deputy are already out looking for her." She waved her hand at the crowd of people. "These folks have offered to search, too."

T.J. looked quickly at the people in the room. He recognized four of his neighbors and a man who worked with his dad. Dane and his family were there and three other boys from his basketball team, standing near a tall officer who was giving instructions.

T.J. went over to them. "Hey, guys," he said. "Thanks for being here. How did you know about this?"

"It was on TV," Dane said.

"I heard it, too," one of the others said, "and I called Jason and Mike. First, we thought we'd be looking for you. Now, we're going to help find your grandma."

"Thanks," T.J. said again.

Dane put his arm around T.J.'s shoulders. "Don't worry," he said. "We'll find her. She'll be OK."

"My son has such wonderful friends," Mrs. Stenson said, to no one in particular. "We all do. Such wonderful friends and neighbors. Look at all these people. Even perfect strangers want to help. A woman who works in a gas station called the police because a boy T.J.'s age had been there earlier, arguing with his father, and when she heard on the news that T.J. was missing, she thought it might have been him." She blew her nose. "Isn't that wonderful, T.J.?" she said. "Someone who has never even seen you was trying to help." She looked around the room and started to cry again.

The tall officer explained that the searchers would work in pairs. "We'll divide this group in half and go both directions on Ridge Road," he said. "At the first cross street, a pair should go in each direction. At the next cross street, another pair goes in each direction. Continue to split up that way and cover as many of the side roads as you can."

The officer emphasized that Grandma Ruth was sick and that whoever found her should immediately report to an officer. "Don't try to move her or make her go with you if she doesn't want to," he said. "She's probably scared already and that might make it worse. If you contact one of us, we can take a family member with us to pick her up and bring her home. Patrol cars will be driving regularly throughout the area so you'll have no trouble finding one of us. When you talk to her, stay calm. Reassure her that she'll soon be home. And remember she is an elderly woman who moves slowly. She's certain to be found within a mile or two."

"What if she's injured?" someone asked.

"What if someone in a car already picked her up?" someone else said.

"What if she runs away when she sees us?"

T.J. cringed. He couldn't stand to listen to all this. He wanted to get on with the search. He left the group and went into the kitchen.

Leaning against the kitchen counter, he drank a glass of water and tried to imagine what Grandma Ruth would have done when she walked away from the Crowleys' barn. Almost certainly, she intended either to come home or to look for David. She would probably not have chosen to walk along a street. More likely, she tried to come back across the field, the way T.J. had taken her to the barn, and then she became mixed up and went off in the wrong direction.

T.J. looked back into the living room. His mother was on the far side of the room, showing a picture of Grandma Ruth to one of the groups of searchers. Her voice sounded too high, as if she might lose control at any moment.

If I tell her what I want to do, T.J. thought, she'll probably say *no*. She'll panic at the idea of me going out alone now, even on our own property.

But he had to go. He couldn't stand around waiting while the authorities gave endless instructions—instructions which did not include searching in the most logical places of all: the field behind the Stensons' house and the Crowleys' pasture.

T.J. scribbled a quick note and left it on the kitchen table. *Mom: I'm looking for Grandma Ruth in our back field.*

He opened the kitchen cupboard and removed the flashlight that his parents kept in case the power went out.

He glanced at his mother one more time before he slipped unnoticed out the back door.

# Chapter Twelve

T.J. started across the field, toward the stand of trees that separated the Stensons' property from the Crowleys'. Walking slowly and looking all around, he retraced the path that he and Grandma Ruth had taken early that evening.

With a pang, he remembered how impatient he had been, how he had resented her dawdling. Why had he thought that watching *Top Gun* was more important than keeping Grandma Ruth happy? If anything has happened to her, he would never forgive himself for being so short-tempered.

"Grandma Ruth?" he called. "Are you here?"

He heard the rumbling of voices behind him as the group of volunteer searchers began to leave the house and head for their assigned areas.

"Grandma Ruth?" T.J. called, louder this time. "Grandma Ruth!" There was no answer.

When he reached the gate that led to the Crowleys' property, he turned back and walked to the opposite corner of the field, in case Grandma Ruth had gone that direction by mistake. He aimed his light back and forth across the ground as he walked. The possibility that she had fallen worried him and he wasn't sure she would respond, even if she heard him call. By now, she might be too frightened and confused to answer. He checked thoroughly all along the strip of shrubs that grew across the Stensons' back fence.

There was no sign of any person in the field so he again walked across the way he and Grandma Ruth had gone earlier. This time, when he reached the gate, he pushed the metal handle to force it open, and entered the Crowleys' pasture.

Salt and Pepper barked loudly as he approached their pen. "Hey, guys, it's me," T.J. called, and the barks turned to excited yips. "Good dogs," T.J. said, as he went by, but he didn't take time to pet them.

T.J. looked in the barn, just to be sure that Grandma Ruth was not asleep somewhere, overlooked by his parents. When he slid open the door, a shiver of fear streaked down the back of his neck. It would be a long, long time before T.J. could step into the Crowleys' barn without remembering how he felt when he first saw Brody.

He wondered what had gone wrong with Brody's mind. Would he be punished for his crimes or sent to a mental hospital?

Sergeant Donnell had said Brody was a victim of society's ills but he could still have helped himself. "Lots of people have setbacks," Sergeant Donnell said. "Life isn't always fair but why waste your time trying to get revenge?"

T.J. turned on the barn lights. Two sleepy kittens stretched lazily.

"Grandma Ruth? Are you in here?"

Quickly, he checked the old horse stalls and what used to be the tack room. Except for the kittens, which rubbed against T.J.'s ankles, mewing hungrily, the barn was empty.

"Sorry this is so late," he said as he poured cat food into the bowl. The kittens munched eagerly.

As he slid the barn door closed, he tried to imagine what Grandma Ruth would have done but it was hard to know. She wasn't in the field, which meant she had either gone down the lane and out onto the street, or she had gone into the woods.

The police and volunteer searchers were looking along all the roads, assuming that Grandma Ruth would walk where it was easy to move, rather than struggling through the woods. T.J. wasn't so sure. Grandma Ruth had always loved to hike in the woods, especially if there was a deer trail to follow. It seemed likely to him that she would avoid the paved roads, if she could. In her confused state of mind, the woods might have seemed the most logical place to go.

T.J. started into the woods.

There had been reports of teenagers in the woods at night, drinking or doing drugs and generally creating a disturbance. People in the Forest View Estates houses on the far side of the woods had complained to the sheriff, who responded by saying it was impossible to patrol every remote section of the county every hour of every night.

Remembering these reports made T.J. even more anxious.

He considered going back and asking Dane to come with him but by now, the volunteers were already dispersed along the roads. If Grandma Ruth had gone into the woods, he didn't think she would be able to go very far; she wasn't strong enough. She moved slowly these days, even indoors, as if she wasn't sure where she was going. It had taken her forever to walk across the field, even with him urging her on, and the woods were much harder to walk in than the field was.

T.J. pushed his way through a thicket of huckleberry bushes. A deep mulch of leaves cushioned his steps. He frequently had to step over fallen branches or work his way around clumps of scrub alder that grew too close together to pass between. He tripped, caught himself, and aimed his flashlight on the ground to see what had tripped him.

It was a blackberry vine, the kind that grows low to the ground and has small, sweet berries. Every summer, until she got sick, T.J. and Grandma Ruth would take a bucket and spend half a morning searching for enough of these berries to make jam.

*Where was she?*

She used to know the woods well. When her brain still worked right, she taught T.J. to recognize the various trees and showed him how the fern seeds grow on the bottom side of the fronds. She taught him the difference between berries that are safe to eat and berries that are not.

More memories flooded T.J.'s mind. He used to watch Grandma Ruth practice the routines from her tap dancing class on the back patio and then she would teach the routines to T.J. until they both collapsed in giggles. He remembered standing on the curb with his mother during a July 4th parade and clapping wildly when Grandma Ruth marched down the street carrying a Humane Society sign that showed a box of kittens and the words THERE'S MORE THAN ONE LITTER PROBLEM.

When she was a school board member, Grandma Ruth sometimes got her picture in the newspaper. T.J. used to clip out the pictures and take them to school. "That's my grandmother," he would brag. The other kids were impressed because his grandmother was important and interesting.

His favorite memories, though, were their picnics in The World's Greatest Outdoor Restaurant. He missed those picnics, although they would have quit going to the willow tree even if Grandma Ruth wasn't sick. When the Forest View Estates housing development was built across the swamp, it made the willow tree easily accessible from that side. It wasn't the same to peer through the circle of branches and see houses in the distance.

A cedar branch brushed across T.J.'s cheek, bringing his thoughts back to the present and the reality of the search for Grandma Ruth.

He stopped. In her illness, Grandma Ruth kept trying to go back to earlier times, to recapture experiences that had made her happy. T.J. had happy memories of the willow tree; maybe Grandma Ruth did, too. Was it possible that, once she found herself in the woods, she would somehow think about The World's Greatest Outdoor Restaurant and make her way there?

He hesitated. In his note, he had told his mother he was searching in their own field. He had already left that and the Crowley property behind. He knew he shouldn't go farther without telling someone where he was going but he was already near the beginning of the swamp. He could hear the frogs, not far ahead.

T.J. decided to take a chance. He knew it was only a hunch but somehow it fit the way Grandma Ruth's mind worked lately. He headed for the swamp. He would check out the willow tree, just in case.

# Chapter Thirteen

T.J. walked faster, now that he had a destination, ignoring the branches that scratched his face. He lifted his feet high with each step, trying not to get tangled in the undergrowth. His legs ached from the effort. His right leg was still sore from when he kicked in the telephone booth and his left ankle throbbed where he had twisted it, running away from Brody. By tomorrow, he would be too stiff to play basketball but the game against Lincoln no longer seemed important.

The ground grew wetter as T.J. approached the swamp. His shoes made a squishing sound and the mud pulled downward as he lifted his feet, slowing his progress. He moved his flashlight back and forth until he spotted the fallen trees that served as a path.

He walked across as quickly as he could without losing his balance, keeping his light pointed downward toward the logs.

As he approached the far side of the swamp, he heard voices ahead.

T.J. switched off his flashlight. If there was a gang of some kind ahead, partying on the dead end street at the other side of the swamp, he did not want them to notice him. He moved more slowly in the dark but he kept going. He couldn't turn back; what if Grandma Ruth was in this vicinity?

When the log path turned left, he looked up and saw light glowing through the thick branches of the willow tree.

The voices were louder now. T.J. paused, trying to hear what they were saying but all he heard was a jumble of laughter. He realized it came from under the branches of the weeping willow tree.

A hollow feeling settled in his chest. He wished that he did not know that drunken rowdies were now using The World's Greatest Outdoor Restaurant as a place to hang out. The knowledge tarnished the image he had of his picnics there with Grandma Ruth. He wanted to keep his memories shiny; he wanted to remember only the happy times at The World's Greatest Outdoor Restaurant.

He should not have come here. Even if Grandma Ruth had wandered this way, she would not go into a group of loud, unfamiliar people. She would turn and go back across the swamp and into the woods. Disappointed that his hunch about Grandma Ruth had been wrong, T.J. turned to sneak away before anyone saw him. As he did, one voice rang out above the rest.

T.J. froze. He would recognize Craig Ackerley's voice anywhere, especially when it had the mean, teasing tone that he always used when he spoke to someone who wasn't likely to fight back.

Craig had said, "What's your name, old lady?"

T.J.'s heart thudded against his ribs and the hollow feeling became a cold ball of fear.

"What's your name, old lady?" Craig repeated. "Don't you know your own name?" His words slurred together and he spoke more slowly than usual.

"Knock it off, Craig," another voice said. "Can't you see she's senile?"

"If she's senile, what's she doing out in the woods alone in the middle of the night?" Craig's voice rose even louder. "I know. She's Little Red Riding Hood's grandmother!" He laughed loudly at his own humor and T.J. heard someone else laugh, too.

"That's right," Craig said. "This is Little Red Riding Hood's little old grandmother, and I'm the big bad wolf."

The drunken laughter seemed out of place under the stately weeping willow, like someone swearing in church.

T.J. moved closer to the weeping willow. He knew from experience that a bully like Craig thrived on an audience. If his companions laughed at him, he would keep on.

"Oh, Grannie," Craig shouted, "what big eyes you have."

"Oh, Wolfie," said another voice, "what a big mouth you have."

Lyle. T.J. was pretty sure the second voice was Lyle Mosser.

"Knock it off," said a third voice.

"Look at these teeth, Grannie," said Craig. "Big bad wolves eat little old ladies like you."

129

T.J. was beside the tree now. A camping lantern lit the circle inside the branches. Through the leaves, T.J. saw Craig and three other boys. Their backs were to him. They faced Grandma Ruth, who stood next to the tree trunk, clutching her purse.

The scene reminded T.J. of an old picture he had seen once in an antique store. It showed a pack of dogs that had a rabbit trapped at the base of the tree. The terrified rabbit's eyes pleaded for help as the dogs bayed triumphantly. T.J. had decided that day never to go hunting, and he had turned the picture face down, hoping no one else would look at it.

Now Grandma Ruth was trapped and her expression was just as frightened as that painted rabbit's had been.

T.J. knew what could happen. He'd seen news reports of drunken thugs who beat up and robbed helpless elderly people. Through the leaves, he wasn't sure who the other boys were but he knew Craig had a mean streak and even people who are good otherwise sometimes do things when they've had too much to drink that they wouldn't dream of doing when they're sober.

He knew he should turn and run. He needed to get help, fast, before Grandma Ruth got hurt.

Yet he didn't move. It would take at least half an hour to get help, if he went back the way he had come. He couldn't leave Grandma Ruth at the mercy of these hoodlums for that long. If he tried to go around the willow tree and run to one of the houses in Forest View Estates, Craig and the others would surely see him and prevent him from getting help.

He stood still, listening. Maybe they would tire of talking

to her, if she didn't respond. Maybe they would decide to leave.

"Let's see what you have in that purse," Craig said.

"Good idea," said Lyle. "Maybe the old dame has some booze money for us."

Craig reached forward and snatched the purse out of Grandma Ruth's hands.

"No!" she cried. "Give me that. The baby needs milk."

Craig's mimicking voice said, "The baby needs milk."

Grandma Ruth began to cry.

Craig opened the purse, looked inside and dumped the Monopoly money on the ground. "Where's the *real* money?" he said.

Grandma Ruth dropped to her knees and began scooping up the play money.

"Maybe we should search her," Lyle said. "Old dames like this sometimes have a lot of dough."

"Good idea," Craig said.

Anger burned inside T.J. and the cold hollow feeling was replaced by a red hot fury.

Craig bent and poked Grandma Ruth's shoulder. "I asked you a question," he said. "Where's your money?"

"Leave her alone!" T.J.'s voice was icy and level as he parted the willow branches and stepped into the circle of light.

The four other boys turned together, the way a flock of birds moves, as if controlled by one impulse. T.J. recognized all of them. He was surprised that the new kids, Allen and Nicholas, were hanging around with Craig. He thought they had more sense than that.

"Well, look who's here," Craig said. "It's Stenson, the English major." His words ran together, as if his tongue was too thick.

"It's time for you and your friends to go home," T.J. said.

"Since when did you give the orders?" Craig said.

"I just started."

"Think again, wimp," Craig said. He hiccuped loudly.

T.J. looked at the other three boys who now stood slightly behind Craig. "Does it make you feel good, to pick on a helpless old woman?" he said. "Real manly?"

The three looked at each other and said nothing. Craig took a step forward, glaring at T.J. He swayed slightly.

"She has Alzheimer's disease," T.J. said, "and she is scared and lost." T.J. looked around Craig, directing his words at the other boys.

Allen and Nicholas looked down at their feet. "We weren't . . ." Allen's voice trailed off without finishing the sentence. Nicholas looked away, refusing to meet T.J.'s eyes.

"What makes you an authority on old ladies?" Craig said.

Grandma Ruth stopped picking up the money and tried to look around the other boys to see T.J. "David?" she said. "Is that you?"

"Yes," T.J. said. "It's David. I've come to take you home."

Craig looked from Grandma Ruth to T.J. and back again. "You know this old dame?" he asked.

"She's my grandmother."

"Why is she calling you David? You got an alias we don't know about?" Craig stepped closer to T.J., the way he always did when he was hassling him.

T.J. knew that Craig was itching to take a swing at him. With three friends to back him up, it wouldn't be much of a match, even with Craig so drunk.

T.J. swallowed hard and looked at Grandma Ruth. She was staring at him, clearly waiting for him to rescue her.

*Use your wits, not your fists.*

T.J. stood tall and looked beyond Craig, at Allen and Nicholas. "I had you two figured to be decent guys," he said. "I thought we might be friends."

"We are decent guys," Nicholas said.

"Then why are you hanging out with scum like this?" T.J. said, pointing to Craig.

"Who are you calling scum?" Craig said.

"He told us it was a party," Allen said. "He said the whole team would be here."

"Don't believe everything Craig tells you," T.J. said.

"Are you calling me a liar?" Craig punched T.J. in the arm.

"Let's just say you know how to stretch the truth."

Allen and Nicholas snickered.

"You're good with words, Stenson," Craig said. "Let's see how good you are with your fists."

"Sorry. I don't want to fight."

"Well, I do." Craig punched T.J. again.

Nicholas spoke up. "Forget it, Craig. We aren't going to have a fight."

"I'm so glad you're here, David," Grandma Ruth said. "I thought I had lost my money." She was still on her knees, picking up the Monopoly money.

Allen began to help her, gathering the money that had scattered the farthest and handing it to Grandma Ruth.

133

"Thank you," she said. "I need this to buy milk for my baby."

"We'll find it all," Allen said. "Don't worry."

"I waited for the preacher," Grandma Ruth said, "but he didn't come." She reached for a piece of green Monopoly money.

"Let's get out of here," said Lyle, as he picked up the half-full wine bottle. "It gives me the creeps, watching her crawl around in the dirt after that fake money."

"She's sick," T.J. said, "and scared."

"There's nothing to be afraid of," Allen said and he patted Grandma Ruth's arm. "T.J. is here and he's going to take you home."

Grandma Ruth looked up at the boys. When she saw T.J., relief spread across her face. "Hello, T.J.," she said.

She knows me, T.J. thought. She remembers.

"Hello, Grandma Ruth."

"Let's go," said Nicholas.

Craig took another step toward T.J. "We can't leave yet," he said. "Stenson's been calling me names."

"When the cops find out you've been bothering my grandmother," T.J. said, "I'll be calling you 'jailbird.' You're going to be in deep trouble."

"Hey, I was only kidding around with the old dame."

"The cops aren't likely to see it that way, and I do have three witnesses."

Craig looked behind him.

"That's right," Nicholas said. "We'll testify."

"Assault and attempted robbery," T.J. said.

Craig took a swing at T.J. but T.J. easily ducked out of the way.

Nicholas grabbed Craig's arm and spun him around. "You're going home," he said. "Now."

"Huh?" said Craig.

"Move," Nicholas said.

Craig moved.

Nicholas looked at T.J. "I'll call the police as soon as I get home, and tell them where you are."

"Do you want me to stay here with you?" Allen asked.

T.J. shook his head. It would be easier for Grandma Ruth if everyone else left. "We'll be OK," he said. "We'll wait right here. It will be faster for someone to pick us up here than for Grandma Ruth to walk back through the swamp and the woods."

"If you're sure you'll be OK," Allen said. "I'll go with Nicholas. He might need me. I'll leave my lantern here for you."

"I don't need it," T.J. said. "I have a flashlight."

Allen patted Grandma Ruth's arm again. "Good-bye," he said. He moved to Craig's other side so that he and Nicholas flanked Craig like a pair of bookends. "Let's go," he said.

"Wait for me," said Lyle. "We never should have come here in the first place. This whole thing was a stupid idea."

"We can't leave!" Craig bellowed. "The party isn't over yet."

"Some party," Nicholas said and he gave Craig another push.

"I like a party as well as the next guy," Allen said, "but

my idea of fun does not include hassling sick old gray-haired women."

"Me, either," said Nicholas.

T.J. gave them a grateful look. He had thought he was going to like Allen and Nicholas; now he was sure of it. Maybe he'd even invite them over for dinner on his birthday, and make his mother happy. They understood that Grandma Ruth was sick. He would have a party and invite Dane, Allen, and Nicholas. He would invite Grandma Ruth to come, too. She would probably love it.

The four boys stepped out from under the willow tree. As their light moved away, T.J. called, "If you ever bother me again, Ackerley, you'll be in juvenile court on charges of molesting an old woman."

"Some people can't take a joke," Craig muttered.

T.J. watched until the group disappeared around a corner, relieved that Craig was going along without any more protest.

T.J. knew he would never again be hassled by Craig. Even when Craig sobered up, he'd leave T.J. alone because Craig would worry that T.J. might really say he had caught Craig robbing Grandma Ruth. Craig was scared of him now and bullies only pick on people they can intimidate. They never go after anyone they're afraid of.

He had won with his wits, not his fists. To be truthful, he had been so angry he would have enjoyed smashing his fist into Craig's stupid face and bopping him on the head with the flashlight but he was glad he had not done it. That would have brought him down to Craig's level and it would not have helped Grandma Ruth. She was frightened enough already; if she had to watch T.J. fight, she would really be upset.

It was dark under the tree, with the lantern gone. Only a little moonlight sifted through the thick branches. He switched on his flashlight and looked at Grandma Ruth. She sat on the ground, twisting her hands in her lap.

Her anxious eyes looked up at him. He could tell she was trembling. He wondered if she was shaking from cold, from fear or, most likely, from both.

"It's all over," he said. "You're safe."

"Is that you, David?" she asked.

"Yes," T.J. said. "It's me." He picked up the last scattered pieces of Monopoly money and put them in her purse. "Come on, Grandma Ruth," he said, holding out a hand. "We're going home soon."

She put her thin hand in his. Gently, T.J. helped her to her feet. Then he put his arms around her and held her close.

A deep love for the Grandma Ruth of his childhood filled T.J.'s heart. He had not realized until that night, when so many memories flooded over him, what an influence she had been on his life. *Wishing won't help . . . win with your wits . . . take action.* For the first time, he appreciated how much she had taught him, how his thinking and personality had been shaped by the person she had been. He knew he would always treasure his memories of that wonderful woman.

But this Grandma Ruth, the here-and-now Grandma Ruth, was special, too, and despite her Alzheimer's disease, he loved her, just the way she was. Never again would he waste time and energy longing for her to go back to her former self. He would quit denying the truth of her disease. He would quit wishing that she wasn't sick and take action to make her happy, if he could, because he loved this mixed-up old woman with her purse full of Monopoly money and her childlike smile, the one who thought he was David.

Her voice quavered against his shoulder. "I waited for you back there, David. I wanted you to come so we could go to church. I was cold but I waited and waited."

"I know. I'm sorry I was late. But I'm here now. We can go to church now, if you want. Would you like that?"

She stepped out of his embrace. A smile spread across her face, erasing the worry lines.

"Will we sing when we get there?" she asked. "Will we sing in the church?"

"We'll sing. We'll sing right now. We don't have to go anywhere else because all the world is our church."

All the world is our church, Grandma Ruth, and every creature has a special place on Earth.

Your words. Your words were right. The lessons you taught me were true.

He took Grandma Ruth's hands in his and began to sing. "Holy, holy, holy."

Grandma Ruth quit trembling. She threw her shoulders back, and joined in loudly.

"Holy! Holy! Holy! Lord God Almighty."

Together, they stood inside The World's Greatest Outdoor Restaurant and sang their joyful hymn.

138